hear me

viv daniels

WORD *for* WORD

Hear Me

Copyright © 2014 by Viv Daniels

Cover photo © prometeus

Published by Word for Word
ISBN: 978-1-937135-14-0

*"From everywhere, filling the air,
Oh! how they pound, raising the sound,
O'er hill and dale, telling their tale."
- The Carol of the Bells*

one

THE CLANGING OF THE BELLS formed a constant din in this neighborhood far at the edge of the town. On the other side of town, where the wide, perfect streets housed the court and the post office and the council hall, you could hardly hear the endless ringing. But all the way out here, where you could see the tops of the forest trees, where cracks in the pavement held the ghosts of gnarled roots, and the residents' hearts still pumped with forest blood, you never escaped the sound of the bells.

You just had to remember that it was for your own protection. The barrier of the bells was the only thing saving the town from the deadly magic that dwelt deep within the forest, magic that could swallow the town whole, along with the soul of every man, woman, and child who walked its streets. For three long years, the barrier—a wall of silver sound twenty-five feet high—had kept the forest out of the town, and the townspeople out of the forest.

A dusting of snow lay on the land like powdered sugar on top of a spice cake. Whenever the wind picked up, it swirled in eddies along the streets, followed by the inevitable racket of the wind-chimed bells. The lattice of bells glowed with power and rang with danger. If you so much as walked on that side of the street, your hair would stand on end and a metallic, acid tang would fill your mouth.

And that was normal people's reaction. Those with magic blood fared far worse.

Every lamppost Ivy Potter passed still held faded, shredding posters of those old days before the bells, a reminder of the time when the forest posed a threat and the town had to fight to save its people. One showed a drawing of a woman in agony, her belly swollen, her legs shackled with vines, standing outside a forest hut while naked, dirty children rolled around in the mud at her feet. *Protect your Daughters! A Forest Life is No Future.* Another was the simple face of a forest man, his ears almost comically pointed, his reddish beard matted. Flowers bloomed in place of his eyes. *Have you Seen this Man? Report Sightings to the Council.*

Grimacing, Ivy pulled her scarf more tightly around her neck and quickened her pace. It was four days before Christmas, and the sidewalks were clogged with shoppers laden with bags of gifts and groceries. To a one, they wore thick, wool hats or earmuffs and kept their eyes averted from the barrier.

Once, tourists had come to marvel at this tiny town at the edge of the wilderness, butting up against the dark forest that nearly filled a crevice between impassable mountains. No matter what changes and advances came to the world beyond, the townspeople here had always kept at least some of the old ways. To outsiders, they were legends at best—rural, backward superstitions. But to the locals, they were a way of life.

Now, these same locals still did a brisk business during the holidays, when the ringing of the bells took on a festive air, and tourists braved the edges of the barrier for glimpses of the monsters that supposedly lived beyond, then scoured the antique shops for relics from the now-forbidden forest.

Her own shop lay on the edge of town, on the very last street before the barrier of the bells. Half flower shop half tea house, Petal and Leaf catered to more locals than tourists. Those who purchased Ivy's rare flowers found them withering the farther they traveled from the reach of the forest, and few tourists had use for her herbal teas.

The locals, however, couldn't live without them.

There was no bell over Ivy's shop door, but every customer looked up when she entered. The relative silence of the shop was shattered by the ringing for an instant every time, as the door opened and broke the green, golden stillness of her haven. The customers, milling as they did among the bottles and plants, or seated at the carved wooden tables, would pause and wince until the door shut again, leaving behind only the whistling of tea kettles or the crackling of the fire.

"It's better in the summer," said one of her regulars, Sallie, to no one in particular. "The leaves muffle it a bit."

The others nodded, as Ivy unwrapped her scarf from around her blonde curls, and hung her coat and hat on a hook by the door. Sallie's observation was no more unusual among her clientele than remarking on a hot summer or a dark winter. In the summertime, when the air was filled with birdsong, the buzzing of insects, and the rustling of tree leaves, you could almost pretend you couldn't hear it. But winter was the worst: the bells pealed all day and all night, with nothing cutting the wind, and nothing to compete with the noise. It filled your head and invaded your dreams.

Those who still had dreams.

Ivy emptied the change she'd brought back from the bank into the cash register, then came around with a fresh pot of redbell tea and refilled Sallie's mug.

"Have another," she said, patting the old woman gently on the arm. "And I don't want you getting up from that table until that crease is gone from between your eyes."

"I'll have more, too, Ivy," said Jeb, another regular. He held up his earthenware cup, his gnarled fingers still wrapped tight around the tea-warmed clay. Ivy brushed a wave of her pale, blonde hair off her shoulders and headed over to refill his cup.

Another woman, a tourist, watched from her table. She sipped gingerly at her mug of peppermint tea; a half-eaten brownie lay on the plate in front of her. "Excuse me," she said to Jeb. "You aren't one of those—do you get the headaches? From the bells?"

He grunted in that particular way you could only accomplish north of sixty, and turned away, revealing the side of his head and the slight arch at the tips of his ears. It was all the answer he'd provide to a tourist, but it was also all she needed.

These days, most of Ivy's local clients were not only part forest folk, they were also elderly. If no history or connections tied you to this dying neighborhood, why stay in a place that made you sick? Almost everyone under fifty was long gone.

Yet Ivy stayed. She stayed for the shop, for the greenhouse her parents had built, and for the plants her father had once so carefully collected from the forest. She stayed for her customers, who wouldn't leave and yet couldn't remain without her herbal tinctures. And she stayed because, bells or no bells, a life out of sight of the forest was unthinkable.

The tourist was taking in her surroundings with new eyes. "So wait, you're *all* descended from...from forest folk?" She glanced down at the brownie with obvious distrust.

"Don't worry about the brownie," something wicked inside Ivy made her say. "That's from the factory across town. But my Peppermint Bliss you've been drinking—well, that should make you sleep a hundred years."

The tourist's mouth dropped open.

"She's joking, ma'am," Sallie said. "That's just an old story. No one here has any magic. We're townies. That's why we're on this side of the bells."

No, no one here had any magic. Occasionally they sported moss-green eyes or pointed ears, but no magic. She and her neighbors with forest blood simply suffered the negative effects of the bell barriers, without any of the perks. Ivy sighed and tipped the teapot toward Jeb's mug, but she was too careless, and steaming liquid sloshed over the side and onto his hand. He hissed in pain.

"Oh, Jeb!" Ivy snatched the towel hanging from her apron and started mopping up the mess. "I'm so sorry! I don't know where my head is today." Setting down her teapot, she rushed over to the window and broke off a piece of aloe from the spiky plant on the sill.

"It's okay, Ivy girl," he said when she returned, but he was clutching his hand and his gruff old face was looking even gruffer. "We know where it is." His gaze shot toward the window, to the lattice of bells on the other side of the street.

Ivy bit her lip. She hadn't figured anyone else was counting days. Then again, tonight was the winter solstice, a hard date to forget for anyone with forest blood.

"Let me see," she ordered, taking his hand in hers. Here were the marks of the life of a carpenter. Old scars from where saws had slipped, a chunk missing from a pinky. In the face of all that, a bit of scalding water wasn't a problem, but she smeared aloe over the affected area nonetheless.

"He was a good man, Ivy," Jeb whispered. "Your pa. Always told me about the best trees in the forest."

Jeb was retired now. Tough to keep woodworking when you had no access to wood. And he and her father had indeed been friends once, when George Potter had scoured the forest for rare specimens and Jeb for fine hardwoods. But that was their old life. The forest was off-limits now, and two years ago tonight, her father had walked right into the barrier and turned into a puff of smoke.

She was still holding his hand. Jeb pulled it back and tsked at her, a hint of mischief on his weathered face. "Now, Ivy, shouldn't you have your hands on a younger fellow?"

"When there are men like you around, Jeb?" she replied, shaking off her gloom. "How can I think of anyone else?"

She returned to the stove to make another pot of her bell tea. *Right, Jeb.* Like there were even any young men around for Ivy to have her hands on. Like there'd been anyone at all that could catch her eye since Archer.

Outside, another gust of wind blew, jarring the lattice of bells and sending ribbons of unease unfurling through half the people in the shop. The edge of a poster whipped back and forth against its lamppost, making the devilish face of the forest man seem to wince in pain.

When Ivy was young, she'd played at her father's side in the forest, and spent many long afternoons and evenings beneath its far-branching trees and among the folk who lived there. Back then, the forest hadn't been seen as a menace. Everyone had heard stories, of course, of things that fed on the night and men who went off into the depths and came back as something other than human. But these dangers were rare and distant, and no one—at least, no one from this side of town—ever gave them much thought. Certainly not Ivy, whose father had worked in the forest, whose mother had come from there.

Back then, the forest folk hadn't seemed so different either. Wilder, perhaps, with little interest in the new types of businesses, transportation, and gadgets that were suddenly available outside the forest. But their forest ways seemed no more magical to Ivy than telephones or credit card machines. They were people, not odd creatures. *People*, like her mother, and like Archer.

Even when they'd been kids, Archer had never cared for Ivy's plastic toys or light up games. He'd taught her to skip stones and climb trees and make slingshots from forked twigs. At Archer's side, Ivy had explored every stream and root and glen between her house and her friend's forest hut. When they'd gotten a little older, they'd explored a lot more than that, and there hadn't been any gadgets involved there either. Little wonder no man had interested her since high school, that she'd never dated Bill Portsman, who drove a bus and asked her out once a season like clockwork, or Shawn Cooper, who used to spitball her hair in math class and now worked at the tire shop. When your first lover could literally read your mind, what hope did any other guy have?

But that was all over now. As the town grew, so did its conflict with the forest, and as they all learned, magic thwarted turns into magic dark. As Ivy became a teenager, the dark magic of the forest began to fight against the encroachment of the town, and as the forest grew dangerous, then deadly, even her forest-loving father had been forced to make a choice.

The wilds of the forest were no longer acceptable to the townsfolk, and the people of the forest even less so. The barrier of the bells had gone up, and Archer and the rest of the forest folk had declined to join the town, choosing the evils they knew of the forest instead of the ones they feared in civilization.

Ivy stared out the window of her shop, at the glowing silver barrier and the treetops beyond. The trees closest to the barrier were dead now, their trunks blackened by invisible fire, their skeleton arms bare even at the height of summer. But farther in, the forest remained wild and deep. Maybe there was a place where the people were safe, where Archer and his kin had carved out a place free from danger.

Or maybe the dark magic her father had feared had consumed them all, and turned the only boy she'd ever loved into a monster beyond reckoning.

two

THE KETTLE WHISTLED ON THE STOVE, its piercing squeal almost soothing next to the constant, bone-deep jangle of the bells. Ivy brushed her thoughts of forest folk away. It was as her father had counseled her in those first horrible weeks, when the sound of the bells had made her neighbors run mad and sent her to bed with earplugs and sedatives that barely took the edge off. He'd told her what she needed to think, the mantra she needed to repeat whenever it all seemed too much to bear.

It does no good to fret about what lies beyond the barrier. I'm safe here in this town. We're all safe, because of the bells.

"I don't understand," the tourist woman was saying now. "If you get headaches from the bells, why don't you leave?"

Ivy rolled her eyes but stayed silent. It all seemed so easy to outsiders.

"Do *you* want to buy my house?" Sallie asked the woman. "It's right by the barrier so it's not like it's expensive. Also, do you know of a good job I could get somewhere else? I'm all ears."

"Pointed ears," Jeb added wickedly, though Sallie, like Ivy, did not have that forest trait.

The tourist scowled into her cup. Ivy already knew what was coming next. "Well, you could go to the forest."

No one could go to the forest, just like the forest folk could no longer leave. The barrier stretched from cliff to cliff in the mouth of the blind canyon, and no one had ever successfully climbed up the sheer sides. The forest was an isolated island of darkness and magic, especially now, cut off from the rest of the world.

And if the folk who dwelled within had succumbed to the darkness since the barrier had been erected, well… they had chosen the forest. Her father had tried to help them. Before the town raised the barrier, he'd gone to the forest folk and begged them to come to the town, where it was safe. They'd stayed on their side.

And Ivy had stayed on hers.

Her life was here, in the town, with the people who needed her. When the neighbor kids moved away for the army or school or just the big cities down the highway and never came back, Ivy stayed. When half the block lay abandoned while people escaped the barrier sickness—until the only ones left were those as entrenched as any forest folk, unable to imagine a life anywhere else but these streets—Ivy remained. Day after day, she tended to the rare forest plants living on in the greenhouse, she brewed her teas, and she served her customers and she listened to the nonstop ringing of the bells.

She flipped the dial on the stove and pulled off the hissing kettle. The recipe for bell tea wasn't difficult, but it was exact. A precise mixture of seventy percent dried petals, twenty percent leaves, and ten percent bulb shavings from the forest redbell flower, plus a few sprigs of mint and holy basil for flavor. The water had to be thirty seconds past boiling, the steeping time, four and a half minutes. Honey was okay, especially local, but sugar dulled the effects. No cream. Never cream.

The dose... well, that depended on the customer. For some, a single cup would do, and she never poured more than four. It wasn't easy to carry the patron home afterwards. Ivy's own prescription was a cup and a half. Sallie had once told her she'd do better with two, especially living so close to the barrier, but Ivy had resisted so far. If she was up to two cups at twenty years old, how many would she be drinking by the time she was her customers' age?

She poured the steaming water over the tea leaves, swirling the pot around to make sure every leaf was saturated.

"Excuse me?"

Ivy jerked her head up to find the tourist woman standing before her. She held a few linen satchels of loose tea. "I'd like to purchase these, please." She smirked. "I mean, if they aren't enchanted."

"They're medicinal," Ivy replied, checking the price tags. "It's up to storytellers to decide how much medicine is magic."

"There's a difference!" the tourist said, indignant. "Magic is, like...evil."

Right. Magic was evil now. Ivy should remember that, especially in front of a stranger. Who knew what stories she'd spread in town about the wicked tea shop owner and her half-fae clientele? Deacon Ryder would wallpaper the neighborhood in posters.

Talk about a headache.

"This tea is Nightmare Eraser," Ivy said, holding up one of the tourist's picks. "It's got chamomile in it for relaxation, lemon balm to soothe your spirits, and anise to repel bad thoughts. You can believe what you want about its potency, but there's nothing in here you can't buy from a grocer's spice rack."

The tourist seemed relieved. She bought the Nightmare Eraser and—to Ivy's amusement—the Love Potion Tea, with its mix of jasmine, ginseng, and rose hips. When she left, Ivy shook her head and entered the purchase in her ledger. She'd told the scared, silly woman the truth. Nothing in the ingredients she sold were magic. If Ivy had a way with plants, that was from her father. And if she had a way with making teas and tinctures… well, she did have her mother's forest blood.

When the headaches had started and too many townspeople had run mad from the sound of the bells, Ivy remembered little from that time except the pain. Headaches so bad you'd vomit and pass out. Sensitivity to everything: the sound of the TV switching on and off made her keel over, the softest setting on the lamp in her room made her cry out in pain. And forget a ringing phone. The ringing bells were more than enough.

One night, in the dark greenhouse, where everything was living and soft and brown, her father explained his discovery. Metal bells had always protected humans from unwanted magic. The bells of the barrier were calibrated against forest magic—evil as well as the good. And she was part forest folk, so the magic was in her blood as well.

Ever since the town's creation, forest folk had worn the redbell flower as protection when they left the woods. All her life Ivy had seen it on them, tucked into Archer's buttonholes whenever he stepped out of the forest, woven into her mother's hair on the few occasions she deigned to visit her daughter. Ivy's father, the botanist, knew it was more than superstition. It was medicine against modernity. He hypothesized that if it couldn't cure the barrier sickness Ivy and her kind suffered from, it would at least mitigate the effects.

"I'm so sorry, Ivy," he'd said, his head bent low over their salvation. "Had I known... I was only trying to protect you."

Yet it was Ivy whose deft hand had perfected the recipe, in materials and technique, and ensured that they could make their tea without destroying their supply of the rare flower.

As long as she took the tea and stayed away from the barrier, she'd be fine. As long as she listened to the town council and trusted that they knew what was best for her and the town, she'd be safe. As long as she tended her garden and brewed her cups and kept her head down, she could pretend that life hadn't really changed so much. That's what her father said to her, every day for months after the bells had started their incessant ringing. It would be worth it, he told her. It would be all right.

She never had discovered why he hadn't taken his own advice.

In the months following his death, she'd tortured herself with hypotheses. Perhaps he'd wandered too close on one of his foraging trips, searching for any rare flora that might remain on this side of the barrier. Unlike those with forest blood, regular people could draw within feet of the bells with little more than a sense of unease and a static shock. It was only touching the bells that caused a zap, like a live wire.

Maybe he found a specimen too perfect to resist. Maybe he thought he could reach through the lattice without touching the lines. Maybe maybe maybe… did it really matter? Now Dad was gone, too.

Her father knew the forest inside and out. He knew the bells would ruin his plant-foraging business. And yet he'd still supported the erection of the barrier. Ivy clung to that knowledge, especially during the first long winter after her father was gone. He, who'd spent his life there, who'd married a forest girl and built a career out of trading the forest folk for ever-rarer specimens of forest flora and loam for his greenhouse. If he thought the forest was threatening the survival of the town, that the darkness within it had grown too great to withstand, then it *had* to be true. As impossible as it seemed, that the forest she'd loved all her life posed a threat to the place she called home… well, her father knew more than her of the dangers in the forest's depths, and he'd seen something that scared him enough to back the council's plan.

Growing up, Ivy had learned from her father how to be responsible and respectful of forest ways and dangers. He was wary, but not forbidding, even after their mother had left them to return to the wild.

"Some aren't meant for a life beyond the trees," he told Ivy whenever she asked why she only saw her mother once or twice a year. He'd reminded her of it again when Archer started coming round. "Are you sure you ought to be spending so much time with that boy, Ivy?" he'd ask, bent over his work desk, his fingers stained green with cuttings. "Don't get too attached. He's forest to the root."

But Ivy had laughed it off. She knew all about Archer's root, after all. And even when the kids at school had snickered behind her back or called her a forest-lover, she hadn't minded. Her father, too, was a forest-lover, and felt no shame. Besides, what was a little town folk prejudice to compare to what she had with Archer?

And yet, in the end, her father had been right, for Archer chose the forest when the barrier went up. He chose the forest over her. Maybe that's why those first dark weeks of bells had been so bad. It wasn't just her forest blood. It was her broken heart.

As the afternoon waned, her customers thinned, exchanging holiday greetings and picking up trifles for their families on their way home. Tonight was the winter solstice, and even those who didn't keep to the old ways anymore wanted to get home before the long night fell. This far north, in the shadow of mountains that scraped the sky, it fell sharp and quick.

The few remaining tourists in the shop finished up their cakes and their Earl Greys and departed, too. Ivy washed the dishes, swept the floor, and loaded up a bag of used linens for the laundry. There were a few busy days left before Christmas, but Ivy had already contacted her regulars and informed them that they were to bring thermoses to tide them over for the holidays. Responsibility was one thing—slavery another.

At last, when it was dark, she collapsed into the sagging corduroy couch in front of the pot-bellied stove, her own mug of bell tea in her hands. Steam wafted up from her cup and tickled her nose as she stared at the glowing coals and yawned. Another year drawing to a close, and still she sat in her father's flower shop, tending to the plants in the greenhouse and brewing tea for her neighbors. She was twenty years old, but aside from no longer going to high school, her life wasn't noticeably different than it was at seventeen.

Wait, strike that. At seventeen, she was at least getting laid.

The first year, it made sense to put off college. Her father had died, and someone needed to man the shop and make the tea for her neighbors. But why was she still here after all this time?

Each autumn she'd resolved to create an exit strategy for the new year, and each Christmas she found herself right here, alone in her shop across from the forest and the barrier, thinking to herself that she stayed in this town not for the things that were here, but for the ones that were long gone.

How many seasons had she spent drifting as near to the barrier as she dared, peering through the jangling, twitching lattice of bells, hoping to learn what was happening in the forest beyond? She never saw anything, magic or otherwise, yet she couldn't break the habit. She had no friends left her age. They'd all moved away, they all thought she was crazy to stick by the bells, like some pathetic victim from the old stories who wasted away when her forest folk lover abandoned her at summer's end.

All the staring, all the waiting in the world wouldn't change a thing. Archer was gone forever, and so was her father. If she was wise, she'd take the hint and leave town as well. If she stayed in the town much longer, she'd wither, sure as the trees planted at the barrier had.

Ivy drank down the last dregs of her cup and nodded to no one in particular. It was settled: come the new year, she'd start making a plan to leave—find a way for her customers to get their tea without her. Maybe Jeb could take over duties in the greenhouse. He wasn't doing much woodworking these days. It would be good for him to have an activity.

And it would be good for her to get away, maybe go to some far off town where bells were forbidden and the forests were friendly. Somewhere where she could study the type of botany that had nothing to do with magic, where no one had ever heard of forest redbell or the tea one might make from it. Ivy used to get good grades in school. She could surely enroll in a college somewhere.

Or maybe just take some time off. A vacation.

Ivy let her head fall back against the cushion of the couch, sighing as the tea dulled the ache winding through her brain. Another place. Tropical, maybe, where all she could hear was the soft whisper of waves against sand and the singing of strange-colored birds, where she could sip frozen drinks decorated with paper umbrellas instead of medicinal tea, where there were new people, maybe even a new man, who didn't remind her of the one she'd lost...

Archer was a vague, blunt emptiness in her chest most days, the twinge of old heartbreak. Rationally, Ivy knew hardly anyone stayed with their first love, and those chances were even more minuscule if your first love was a mercurial, half-wild forest boy. She only had to look at the example of her own family, at her forest mother, who'd rather range the depths of the wilderness than get stuck with anything so mundane as child rearing. Forest lovers weren't for keeps, no matter what pretty promises they made you as they took off your clothes.

But, oh, those memories. Ivy stretched on the sofa, smoothing her hands down the length of her sweater and feeling her flesh tingle with sudden warmth. Yes, most days, Archer was nothing more than an old ache, but there were nights when her head filled with images and her body with sensations she couldn't quell, even with all the redbell in her father's greenhouse.

The first time they'd slept together, it had been high summer in the forest, and Archer had built her a bower of branches and flowers, high in the limbs of an ancient forest tree halfway between his village and the border of Ivy's town. Midsummer's night bonfires burned bright in the forest, and the sound of forest drums and reed flutes made every leaf and twig tremble beneath their magic. Despite a lifetime of wandering forest villages, sixteen-year-old Ivy had been scared. Children weren't allowed at the rites, and now that she was of age, Ivy quickly understood why. The gossip she heard in town finally made sense, as the savagery and wildness of forest folk was revealed to her in all its naked—literally—glory.

Earlier, she'd begged her father to let her stay, and now she was wondering if perhaps she should have gone home. And then Archer had come for her. Archer, her old friend, who'd lately made her heart

19

beat faster every time he came close, and blush whenever he'd whispered in her ear.

"Ivy." The whisper in her ear was louder than all the drums in the forest. She could hear it in her bones. Archer had drawn her away from the flames and whispered of secret surprises to show her. So they'd left the bonfires behind. She'd trembled with fear and anticipation as she climbed up into the tree he'd brought her to, and gasped with shock and pleasure when she'd come upon the bower.

"Do you like it, Ivy-mine?" he'd asked, almost bashfully, his cheeks pink in the white light of the summer moon.

She'd loved it. She'd loved him, and nothing in the world felt more right than to bare herself to him, body and soul, in the middle of the forest night.

You weren't supposed to keep your first love, no matter how your body burned for his touch. You weren't supposed to yearn for a boy who'd never pick you over his wild forest home. And you were never, ever supposed to wish that things had been different, that the barrier separating you had never gone up. That way lay madness, and magic, and the destruction of your whole town.

Ivy knew better. She swore she did. But as her eyes grew heavy and the flicker of the fire blurred before her eyes, she couldn't help but wonder. Would it be worth it to be swallowed whole by dark magic, if it meant one more night with the man she loved?

~

Ivy wasn't woken by the stinging zap of static that momentarily engulfed the town, that made the lights flicker and the street signs tremble and buzz. She didn't notice when her clay pots rattled on their shelves or her glass vials jingled in their holders.

Rather, it was the nothingness that followed which brought her to. Her eyes flashed open and she sat up, as if from a nightmare she couldn't remember, so disoriented by... something... that for a moment she wasn't even sure where she was. This was home—her shop, her couch, the fire burned down to soft, pink embers. But there was still... something. Something missing.

She stood, by instinct putting out her hand to help her balance, but there was no rush of dizziness, no twinge of constant pain as there'd been for three years. She froze as the truth hit her in a silent wave.

The bells had stopped.

three

SCARCELY DARING TO BREATHE, Ivy tiptoed to the front door of her shop. She peered out into the darkness. It had snowed again while she dozed, and the formerly speckled street lay beneath drifts of frothy white. The bulb of every streetlight had blown, casting the entire street in blue-black shades of midnight. And across the way, the lattice of the bell barrier stood, still, silent—*silent*—and almost invisible. There was no jangle, no buzz of power, and the metal of each tiny alarm was dull and dead.

The barrier was down. The forest lay open, for the first time in years. Ivy swallowed, fear and relief waging war in her soul.

She should pick up her phone. She should call the town council. The barrier was failing.

She should put on her warmest coat and sprint for the forest before it was too late.

In the end, she did neither, for something moved, there in the darkness. At first, she thought it was just another drift of snow, but then it shifted and groaned and the snow shuddered off a lump of bloodied flesh the shape of a man. Heedless of the winter night, she slipped her feet into her boots, opened the door, and crossed the street.

This is dark magic, said something in the back of her head. *Run. Scream.*

But Ivy's father had died at the barrier, and maybe this person was about to die now, so she walked ever closer.

The lump moved again, and grunted. She reached it and the form was unmistakable now. A man—a young man, his naked, blood-smeared back a mass of corded muscle, his tousled, too-long hair the color of late autumn leaves. She knew the back, she knew the hair, and she knew the man lying in the snow.

Ivy could no longer feel the cold.

"Archer," she whispered, but Archer did not move again.

She rushed to his side and knelt in the fresh powder. This close, she could smell copper and ashes, and when she reached for him, blue-black sparks arced between her fingertips and his skin. She shrank back and toed his form with the rubber sole of her boot. He grunted, but did not wake.

He was not dead, then. Not yet. She reached out her hand again. His body sizzled beneath her hand, like the worst static shock, but that was all. Ivy looked up and down the deserted street, searching another witness to her discovery, but there was no one. Just she and Archer, and a wall of silence, and the black forest beyond.

Ivy shuddered. Anything could be lurking there, just beyond the shadows of the trees. She should get inside. But she wasn't leaving him here, half naked in the snow. Forest men were tough, but they still needed coats in wintertime.

It wasn't easy to haul a shirtless, freezing man back into her shop, but somehow Ivy managed it. She stoked the fire in the stove, put a kettle on to boil, and pulled out every blanket she owned. Getting him warm was the first step, and then she'd see about getting him conscious.

With efficiency born of thousands of days in the shop, she moved quickly, gathering supplies from her collection of creams and tinctures to tend to his wounds. She piled the blankets at the foot of the couch and straightened, looking at her charge in the light of the fire.

Archer, lying before her, like a vision out of her wildest dreams.

Or her worst nightmares. The red abrasions fanning across his back and arms didn't look like burns—not exactly—but she knew what happened when one attempted to breach the barrier. He was lucky he escaped with mere burns.

Or was it luck? Her father had burned to a crisp, and he didn't even have the magic the barrier had been erected to thwart. For a full-blooded forest man to withstand it must have been nearly impossible. And she could barely contemplate what it must have taken to stop the bells altogether.

The silence scared her. She could hear herself breathe; she could hear *him* breathe. How long had it been since she'd heard something as simple as the rhythm of another person's breath, unhindered by the endless jangle of bells?

And what sort of danger had Archer been in that braving the barrier seemed like the better choice?

Once, she might have known from Archer, from the mere touch of skin on skin. Though Ivy's mother had been forest folk, she'd inherited little of their magic. Still, Archer could always bring it out of her. When he held her hand, he could share a memory. When he'd kissed her, she could see flashes of his thoughts. And when they'd slept together, back in those slow, summer days when their lives seemed as full and endless as the forest itself, their very souls seemed to link up.

When Ivy had tried to explain it to her town friends, they ridiculed her for falling prey to forest tricks. When she'd ventured to confess to a forest girl, she'd responded as if Ivy had been awed by the intricate mysteries of breathing or digestion. Archer himself had laughed.

"Ivy," he'd sighed as he slipped off her dress. "Oh, Ivy-mine. Of course we're linked. Didn't you know? You and I share a single soul."

But Archer had been wrong. For the barrier had gone up and they'd both gone on, alone, and for two people with a magical shared soul like he claimed, she'd felt awfully isolated these past three years. If they were truly so in sync, wouldn't she have known he was alive? Wouldn't she have instantly realized the bloody lump in the snow was the body of the only man she'd ever loved?

No, it was just a lie for young men to tell their lovers in the dark, just a bit of forest trickery, like the townsfolk said. A forest man could show you plenty of pretty fantasies to get you into bed. Weren't the forest-blooded residents of the town enough evidence of that? They were all products of short-lived flings with forest folk. Ivy and her father had been abandoned by Ivy's forest folk mother as soon as she realized that dull townie life and child-raising weren't to her wild taste.

As a teen, Ivy hadn't cared about that. Archer was excitement and awakening. Loyalty and responsibility existed only in some distant, grown-up world.

She knew better now. Ivy unfolded the first of the blankets and got to work. The first step, unfortunately, would be his pants. The buckskin trousers were soaked and stiff with blood. They'd have to come off. She clenched her jaws and tugged at the fastenings, keeping her eyes averted as they popped free and his pants peeled away from his skin. She closed her eyes and pulled them down, but they caught.

Of course. She opened her eyes and tried to maneuver the pants around his butt and crotch, trying not to let her eyes linger too long on unfamiliar scars trailing down his torso and legs and the all-too-familiar other parts, which were shadowed by far more hair than she remembered him having at sixteen.

Cut it out, Ivy. He's unconscious and wounded. Stop staring at his cock.

She washed the lingering dirt and debris from his body, but when her fingers brushed his skin, she felt nothing otherworldly at all. No whisper of dreams or glimpse of what might have transpired at the barrier to bring it down and him across. Maybe the magic had always been Archer's alone, and he'd merely indulged her with tiny moments back when she was sharing his bed. After a few more minutes, she gave up trying to peer into his soul, applied antiseptic and bandages, then covered him head to foot in blankets warmed near the fire.

Was anyone else awake on this long, dark night? Did the others know the barrier was down? Again, she thought she should warn someone. They could post guards, perhaps, until the town council figured out how to reinstate the bells.

She shuddered at the thought. The silence had barely lasted half an hour, yet the idea of the bells now seemed the worst violation imaginable. Every cell in her body rebelled against the idea. For three years, she and her neighbors had suffered for the town's safety. One night couldn't hurt, could it?

Besides, if the cessation of sound had disturbed her, it must have woken everyone on this side of town. It must have shocked the night guards at the quarry. They would have heard it, though, not felt it, since quarry workers were always townie, born and bred. Ernest Beemer, the quarry owner, liked it that way, and besides, no one with forest blood wanted to work the cliffs so near the power station. But someone there must have contacted authorities. They were on it. They didn't need help from a twenty-year-old florist. Her first duty was to help Archer.

As quietly as possible, she moved around her shop, warming broth and water in case Archer was hungry when he woke. He'd need pain relief, most certainly. Unthinking, she reached for her tin of bell tea, then almost laughed. No one would need a dose tonight.

Cocoa. The memory came back like the snap of a slingshot. As a child, Archer had been obsessed. To a forest boy, chocolate might as well have been the most exotic substance on Earth. He hadn't cared for cars or video games, could barely remember the words for TV or telephone, but boy, had he loved candy.

She closed the tea cabinet and reached for her baking supplies. Cocoa powder, milk, sugar... a dash of vanilla, a pinch of cinnamon. She put a spoon to her lips and smiled. Gone were the days when the best she could provide for her friend was a packet of pre-mixed, chocolaty chemicals.

Mid-whisk, Ivy shook her head. The barrier of the bells was down and Archer was lying naked and wounded on her couch, and here she was thinking about the relative quality of instant versus homemade cocoa.

There was a groan from the vicinity of the couch. Ivy poured the frothy cocoa into two mugs, set them on a tray, and carried it back to where she'd left Archer.

His eyes were still closed, and his chest rose and fell evenly. She put down the tray and looked at him in the firelight. The straight, slashing line of his brows cut deep shadows across his face. His reddish brown hair tangled in waves on his forehead and down his neck, curling around ears which featured the slight point that often appeared on forest folk. His full lips were slightly parted in sleep, and a scruff of hair framed his wide mouth and hid the tiny cleft in his chin. She'd never seen Archer with a beard before. She doubted the teenage version could have grown one. His hair was redder there, as it had been near his groin.

Ivy bit her lip. She really shouldn't be thinking about his groin.

He'd brought the smell of the forest with him. It filled her little shop with scents she hadn't known in years—wood smoke and ancient pine, creek moss and loamy rot.

Beneath his lids, were his eyes the same cheery, gray-green of mossy stones, or had they been replaced by dark-hearted violets, like the men in the posters? Was he as quick to laugh, or had three years trapped in a forest full of evil magic squeezed the humor out of him? There were scars on his body—old scars she had no memory of, scars that spoke to battles and hardship he and his people could not escape. He was thinner than he'd been as a boy, but harder too, his adolescent softness giving way to sinew and bone.

His eyes began to flutter as he slipped into a dream. Ivy watched him in silence. It hadn't worked last time, when she'd been cleaning him up, but maybe he'd been too deep in unconsciousness then. Maybe there'd been nothing to see. She reached a tentative hand toward his chest, her fingers spreading wide over the planes of his ribs and pectoral muscles, as if, through the layers of muscle and bone, she might hold his heart. She felt its thump beneath her palm, a firm, steady drumbeat. How she'd loved to do this on a summer night when they lay wound together, naked and sweaty, surrounded by leaves and the song of crickets and the sparkle of...

Moonlight.

Magic wrapped round her fingertips and pulled her into Archer's visions.

Moonlight gleamed silver off the edge of the bells, which shone like knives hung in neat, unnatural rows. The trees nearest the abomination moaned and creaked, dead branches swaying on dead trunks, dead roots still clinging to dead earth. If there was anything to see on the other side, it was impossible to tell. Pain and death and terrible enchantments flowed from the bells in waves, pounding, ringing, clanging, shrieking.
Ever closer, ever larger, ever louder.
Ivy Ivy Ivy. Bells Bells Bells.

A hand closed tight around her wrist and she gasped, opening her eyes to find Archer staring right at her, his eyes a pure, unending black, his mouth a straight, unreadable line.

"Why," he said roughly, "if it isn't Ivy Potter, all grown up." Then he yanked her close and pressed his mouth to hers.

four

IF IVY ACTUALLY HAD BEEN WAITING three years to feel Archer's lips once more, she would have been vastly disappointed. For this was no tender, affectionate kiss, nor a passionate, crushing possession of her mouth. He neither caressed her nor devoured her, but it didn't matter. It wasn't about their lips or their history—it was about magic. A stampede of images trampled through Ivy's head, obliterating every other sensation.

Abandoned forest villages, their simple huts collapsed in decay. Sickly children writhing on cots in dark corners, the sad, weary eyes of a young woman.

"The darkness is spreading, Archer."

Dry creekbeds and blackened clearings. Redbell flowers crushed in mud, the sting of blood in eyes, the mangled head of a deer, strange symbols carved into its hide. A blood-soaked Archer lifting the head high by the antlers as viscera streamed like water from its severed neck... and the woman's voice again.

"It must be stopped, or we'll lose them all."

Abruptly Archer pulled away from her and spat on the floor. "You taste of plastic," he said with a grimace.

Ivy stumbled backward a step, and raised her hand to cover her lips, her senses still reeling with the memories he'd shared. Death and agony, and that strange forest woman. But she shouldn't be surprised. There was no reason to think he'd been pining for *her*.

She hadn't been waiting for him. She *hadn't*. She never even thought she'd see him again. Ivy glanced down at the tray sitting on the coffee table, at those two pathetic mugs. Cocoa. How stupid could she be? They weren't children anymore.

Archer was sitting up now, the blankets fallen from his broad shoulders and sagging around his hips. Her gaze widened. His eyes were green and mossy again. Had it been nothing but a trick of the light?

"I see you wasted no time taking off my clothes." He eyed her wryly. "Where are my pants, Ivy Potter?"

She sank to the chair opposite him without taking her eyes off her visitor, lest his face change again. "Drying. What are you doing here?"

He shook his head, that inscrutable smile still playing about his lips. "That isn't the question you want to ask."

It was one of the questions. One of a million. They rushed on her like an avalanche, threatening to bury them both alive. "How did you pass through the barrier? Are you the one who broke it, or was it broken by dark magic?"

He smirked at her and his eyes flashed from green to black in the flickering firelight. "Yes."

A chill of horror flooded through her, and Ivy crossed her arms over her chest and shivered, despite the heat pouring out of the stove, despite Archer's kiss. The truth of her situation was suddenly, perfectly, terrifyingly clear.

The barrier was down. The barrier erected to keep the town safe from dark magic. The barrier her father had insisted was necessary, *absolutely* necessary to their survival, though it would separate him from his life's work, and her from her lover, forevermore. The barrier was down, and she'd taken the first thing to come from the forest in three years and put it *in her house*.

She opened her mouth to speak, but her throat had gone dry. Her mind reeled with every story the town council had reported of the darkness of the forest, of the children with no heartbeat and the men with eyes of stone and flowers. Always she'd thought it was real—that monsters *looked* like monsters. But what if the darkness burned from within, a fever you didn't notice until it roasted you alive?

She swallowed, and dared to speak. "Archer?"

"Ivy?" was his only reply. Those pure black eyes were looking at her, his expression amused, but there was danger in it, too. When she'd pulled him inside, all she'd seen was Archer, the boy she'd trusted as long as she could remember. But this man in front of her was someone different. A stranger, like the faces on the posters, his eyes odd with enchantment. The man in the vision, the one nearly black with blood, the one who'd knifed runes into the head of a deer— who was that? What else had he done?

He looked like himself — or a twenty-one-year-old version, anyway. Everything she had once imagined he would grow into. What if it was a lie? What if brambles gnarled beneath those reddish curls, if icemelt flowed through his veins instead of blood? What if the being before her was never Archer at all?

She searched his face for answers, but there were none. With every breath, with every blink, he changed — the man she'd loved, a monster she'd never met. Her fear grew large, like a giant bubble within her, threatening to pop from her skin. Her gaze shot to the door and when she looked back, he gave her a nearly imperceptible shake of his head.

"I'm not so injured that I cannot stop you before you reach that door."

She knew that truth well. Even the old Archer could beat her at a footrace, in forest or in town. He wasn't a ranger like his brother or her mother, but he was faster than a botanist's daughter. Whatever he was now, she knew he'd catch her. "And what if I scream?"

He cocked his head. "To whom? You have no man. I'd smell him on you."

She blinked and hugged herself tighter. "You would not."

"Have you forgotten so much?" His smile showed teeth now, and Ivy's blood ran cold. "Apparently you have."

Odd. Looking into the face of dark magic, Ivy felt like she'd forgotten way more than that. Her memories of the dangers of the forest had dimmed, and she'd cherished and replayed the ones that had remained, memories of light and happiness and love.

But maybe everyone in town was right. The forest was deadly—and Archer was forest.

She dashed for the door, and he sprang into action, grabbing her from behind. His arms snaked about her waist, lifting her up off the floor. She kicked her legs in vain and felt his muscles bulging as he squeezed her tight enough to make her gasp.

"Stop squirming, you townie fool!" he hissed in her ear. "I'm not going to hurt you."

Her arms were trapped at her sides, and her hands brushed his bare thighs. Oh, right, he was still naked. Naked and pressed up against her, his skin hot enough to scorch through several layers of clothes. She had to get away now, before things got completely out of hand.

She closed her eyes. *Just do it, Ivy.* She reached back, found his balls, and squeezed... hard.

He dropped her.

And instead of running, she turned to look at him, standing there, his hands cupped protectively around his manhood as he glared at her. His eyes, thankfully, looked human again. Human, and filled with rage.

"I *said*," he growled, "that I wouldn't hurt you."

"*I* didn't say anything." She straightened, her stance a challenge.

"So you want me to leave?" He spread his hands and she averted her eyes, all too aware of the irony. She wouldn't look at it, but she'd crush it with her bare hands. "Bring me in, patch me up, kick me out into the snow?"

"When I carried you in, I didn't know you'd torn down the barrier with dark magic," she replied. She'd thought he was the man she'd been holding a torch for all these years, not some kind of evil sorcerer with a crop of forest children.

He threw back his head and laughed. "You *are* a fool. What can fight dark magic but more of the same?"

And what was that supposed to mean? Ivy could hardly think with him standing there, magnificently naked and completely uncaring. She grabbed his still-clammy pants off the radiator and threw them at him. He flinched as if she'd lobbed a weapon in his face, instead of damp and dirty clothes.

"I don't know what you are." Ivy hated the unmistakable catch in her voice.

"I'm not surprised."

He snatched the pants off the floor and considered them for a moment, as if they were alien. He looked at her and she kept her gaze at chest level and above, and then, with an expression of amused concession, he slipped them back on without taking his eyes off her. She couldn't tell if that was to ensure she wouldn't run or simply to unnerve her.

Once he looked proper again, he straightened, spreading his arms in a shrug. "I hardly know anymore either."

Her eyes narrowed. Would dark magic say something like that? "I mean, are you Archer, or are you some dreadful thing made to look like him?"

"I ask myself that every day."

"That's not an answer."

"Is it not?"

A sob strangled in her throat. She would not relent. Not until she knew what she was dealing with.

"Where is your father?" he asked.

"What," she tossed at him, mockingly, "you can't smell him?"

Archer said nothing and after a moment where his gaze seemed to worm through her skull, she lowered her eyes.

"He's dead. Two years ago this week." What might her father be able to glean from Archer, or not-Archer?

"I'm sorry." He bowed his head for a moment, then looked back up at her. "But someone continues his work. You know the way to withstand the barrier's curse. I tasted redbell on you."

"Really?" she snapped, almost angry that he assumed she had nothing to do with her tea. "Beneath the plastic?"

"Oh, I tasted all kinds of things beneath the plastic, Ivy Potter." The smile played across his lips again, and this time, it wasn't quite so scary. "There was also cocoa."

She rolled her eyes and pointed at the table. "It's right there."

"You made hot cocoa for me? And you thought I was a—how do you townies put it?"

"Soulless monster," she intoned. "And, like I said, not when I made it. Drink your chocolate and leave." Did monsters like hot cocoa?

"Always a gracious host." He strode over to the tray and lifted the mug. "You made two. Shall we share?"

The words sounded inviting, but Ivy knew better, even as her heart ached. He didn't mean it, no matter how much he sounded like the boy she'd known.

"Have both," Ivy said stiffly. "I'm a very gracious host."

He put the mug to his lips, and as he began to drink, Ivy felt like she could taste it, too, the rich, creamy froth flowing over his tongue and down his throat, warming him up from the inside out. He was wearing pants now, but he might as well still be naked for all the difference it made to Ivy's imagination. She couldn't take her eyes off the line of his spine, at the way his muscles slid beneath his skin as he downed his cocoa.

But now was her chance. His back was to her, his attention diverted. She took a single step backwards.

"Ivy," Archer warned. "Don't. I have eyes in the back of my head."

"Real ones?"

He swept his hand through his ruddy hair. "Come and see."

Gross. "No, thank you."

Archer chuckled and started in on the second cup, and this time, when Ivy caught the taste of cocoa on her tongue, she knew what it was. Magic. Archer—or whoever this was—didn't even have to touch her now to make her feel what he wanted her to. What had he done to steep such strong enchantments? Was this what happened when a forest man's magic went dark?

She should really call the council.

"And you can forget about using your... cellaphone?" He held up her phone.

Her hands flew to her pocket. When had he slipped it out? When they kissed? When he grabbed her? And how had he known what she'd been thinking? No, this was not the Archer she remembered.

Though he still couldn't pronounce the words of the modern world.

"These things are bigger than I remember."

Once, Ivy had laughed at such statements, but she didn't feel like laughing now. "Smarter, too."

He looked down at the bit of glass and plastic in his hand. "Not smart enough, it seems." He put it back in his pocket, though he grimaced as he did. She imagined it must burn, as there wasn't a scrap of redbell on him tonight. No protection from the bells, no protection from the town.

"What happened to you?" She didn't like the tremble in her voice, but there it was. If she couldn't run, she might as well slake her curiosity.

"In three years in the forest? What hasn't happened?" He shrugged, still facing away from her. "Let us play like in the old stories, Ivy Potter. You can ask me three questions, and I'll tell you whatever you wish. Starting now."

Questions blossomed in her brain, so many they threatened to choke out every other thought. Was he the Archer she remembered, or had he been turned by dark magic into... something else? If he'd harnessed something evil to bring down the barrier, why? What had he been doing all this time? What had become of the forest? Who was the woman in his mind's eye, the one with the dark hair and the overwhelming sadness and the small, sick children?

Now Archer turned around, his eyes as dark as onyx, and Ivy tensed again. Some deep, primal part of her cried out to run. This was a fox, and she was a rabbit. Not quick enough and, like her phone, not smart enough either.

"I hardly need to warn you, though," he added, "that we forest folk are tricky."

No, Archer. He didn't need to warn her. She'd already learned her lesson about that.

five

"I DON'T WANT TO PLAY GAMES WITH YOU,"
Ivy said.

"Lies." His eyebrows quirked, a mix of humor
and menace, and he blinked his eyes green. "You're
dying to know everything. I tasted that in your kiss as
well."

"Is that why you k—" she cut herself off,
because she remembered the rules from the old
stories. Three questions. She would not waste them.

Archer was facing her fully, now, and the look he
was giving her was superior and cocky,
Rumplestiltskin and Pan. Pan, especially, given his
bare, muscled chest. He hadn't had those abs at
sixteen either.

Ivy clenched her jaw. But she could do this. She
just had to be careful and clever and brave. She could
be Puss in Boots; she could be Jack the Giant-Killer.
She knew all the rules. Her father had taught her

when she was just a girl, and her father knew everything about the forest.

The coals glowed merrily in the stove. It had started to snow again outside, fat flakes drifting past the window. And the silence—the glorious *nothing* in the air. Her ears and head and heart were full of it. For the first time in years, she could think without the ringing.

She could do this.

"You're wilder than you were before," she said at last.

"That is not a question."

"It's an observation." Ivy circled the couch, watching him. He tracked her with lichen-green eyes, his muscles tensed like an animal ready to spring. "And it's true. You never used to put so much stock in the old stories, the old ways of forest folk."

The Archer she'd known had been gentle, kind, and understanding of the thing that made Ivy a girl from town. When other forest men were roughly taking their lovers before midsummer fires, Archer had made her a canopy of flowers, a bed of petals, and a night of kisses. It was his first time, too, but he still took care, and created a night that worked for her as well as him. And in the magical year that followed, he may have been as wild as the forest night, but was still as sweet as summer sun.

But this Archer? This one was a mystery. She didn't know what to ask that would get her the answers she wanted. She didn't even know if she wanted them. For years she'd told herself that Archer was well, in the forest, even if she'd never see him again. But what if this was the truth? Archer, turning to another woman. Archer, cursed, devoured by the darkness.

If Ivy were the one he'd been with all those years, she never would have let this happen to him. Whoever this forest woman was, Ivy hated her.

"Are you asking me if it's a product of living only in the forest for all these years or if it's dark magic what stole my soul?" His eyebrows lifted in amusement, but Ivy didn't feel amused.

"I haven't asked a thing." She'd *wondered*, yes, but she wouldn't waste a precious question on a simple either-or.

If Archer were playing by fairy story rules, she'd have to be very clever. If he'd fallen to darkness and left a monster to wear his skin, she'd have to be cleverer still.

Ivy took a deep breath. *Think, think.* "What is the full story of the most significant event to transpire in your life since the barrier was erected?"

His eyes never left her face, but she saw the fear behind his gaze. It flashed for only a second, but it was there. Which meant Archer might be, too. Ivy hardly dared to hope.

After a long silence, he spoke. "It was the first morning in your cage. High summer. Glorious sun, trees in full leaf. I left my village to come to our tree…"

She looked away. She'd been locked in her room, safe in her bed, and he'd been at the barrier. Had he been coming for her? Too late, but coming all the same.

"As I walked closer, I heard them. Your silver bells."

She wished he'd stop calling them hers. She hadn't wanted the barrier. She'd hated it every day. The bells had killed her father, made her skin crawl, kept her from Archer… they weren't *hers*.

"They filled the air," Archer said, "setting everything on fire. The trees, the soil. But I kept walking. My blood boiled beneath my skin. My face blistered, my bones crumbled."

Stop. Heat traveled along her own skin, sizzling like fire ants and ashfall. Was this magic, like with the hot chocolate? Was he doing this to her? He didn't even need to chase her, if he could hurt her from afar.

"With every clang, my flesh shuddered so hard I thought it would collapse, that I'd dissolve entirely and turn into mush where I stood." She looked back and he was still staring at her, his expression accusing, and swirling back to black. "And still I walked."

"Stop!" She couldn't take it anymore. Not the magic and definitely not the story. Not the memory of Archer, *her* Archer, coming for her.

He merely shrugged as his eyes were swallowed up by darkness again. "You asked."

She had. And this was his response, to burn her with dark magic. After this, she'd need no more reminders of who her Archer had become. She stared at him, his blackened eyes, as if to force herself to believe it. "Fine."

"It's the end of the story, anyway. I don't remember reaching the barrier, but I'm told that's where they found me. I don't remember anything for weeks. When I woke, I was lying in a bed of redbells, and summer had passed. We were alone in the forest, and it wasn't just the year that was dying."

"And so you decided to turn to dark magic?" She clapped a hand over her mouth. *Dammit.* She'd been so careful, too.

"No," he replied, and a secretive, scary smile curled his lips. "That decision, alas, was made for me." He didn't elaborate. He didn't need to, by rule. She could have cut out her foolish tongue.

"One more, townie."

"Stop calling me that."

"Is it not true?" He cocked his head. "Where have you been these three years if not this town?"

Ivy's head snapped up. *Well, well, well.* That was unexpected. "Those are your first two questions to me."

For a moment, he looked shocked, but it gave way to a grin far kinder than the enigmatic smiles that had come before. "Well done, Ivy."

Ivy, now? Not the sneering *townie* or even her full name, hurled like an epithet? That was unexpected, too. She swallowed, once again unsure. Was he playing with her? A forest man wouldn't so easily give up those questions. A creature of darkness, even less likely.

So then why would he let questions slip from his lips? Was there a trick in them that she didn't know? Or was she, as he said, playing well?

"Perhaps I'm not so very townie after all."

He conceded with a nod. "So give me your answers."

She thought carefully, trying to figure out his trick and learn what info he was trying to glean. "It's not true. I have lived in this town, in this building, across from these bells, but it does not define who I am. It doesn't define any of us, unlike the forest folk,

45

who would rather risk death than live anywhere else but the dark forest."

"What makes you think that?"

It was Ivy's turn to smile. "Question three."

He scowled now, and Ivy couldn't help but thrill at it. She breathed true for the first time since she'd first caught a glimpse of his cursed eyes. She *was* the hero of an old story. She knew what she needed to know and she hadn't even used her third question. Dangerous he might be, and even dark with magic, but—thank heaven, if heaven there was—he was still Archer.

His sly, tricky forest folk demeanor was a mask he wore, and everything else—well, he was just trying to scare her. A monster wouldn't ask questions about her past. A monster wouldn't care so much what she thought. A monster wouldn't have gulped down her cocoa like it was going out of style. He was a man, not a monster.

But that didn't mean she could trust him.

"I think it," she exclaimed, "because you forest folk didn't leave the woods when you had the chance. You knew there were dangers. We warned you, and you chose to stay — your lifestyle was far more important to you than your safety." She gestured at him. "Look how well that's turned out."

He glared at her, his jaw tight, every muscle in his arms and shoulders tensed. Every trace of humor, every shade of humanity, every detail that had convinced her that—whatever else had befallen her friend—he was still the Archer she'd loved as a teen, had left his face, leaving nothing but fury behind.

"Don't kid yourself," he said. "You're a townie, root to stem. And you know *nothing*. You sit here day after day and you put your flowers in their little plastic prisons, as if they are yours to own, to live or die as you see fit. And your town did the same to us with their hellish cage of bells."

"We had to protect ourselves!" she cried. "It's not our fault you wouldn't leave! It's not our fault you didn't care enough to save yourself from dark magic."

His brow furrowed. "Don't speak to me of dark magic, Ivy Potter." He pointed behind her, toward the door and the street and the forest beyond. "That barrier is the blackest enchantment the forest has ever known. Believe me when I tell you that the blackest of magics are those that men wrought themselves. Whatever evils are in the depths, they have been there longer than history's telling, longer than towns or villages or men and women. They belong to the Earth the same as you and me. Those bells of yours are evil of a different sort. There is nothing in the forest that can compare, and nothing that poses so dire a threat."

"Not true!" Ivy exclaimed. They'd been bombarded with stories in those final weeks before the bells had gone up. Terrible beings, excruciating curses, babies and families and lives lost to enchantment. Even her father had told stories of the horrors he'd seen, there in the town square, on the podium where all could see and hear. And Ivy had stood in the square and listened, her skin crawling as she remembered the nights she'd spent in Archer's bower, high at the top of a forest tree, her heart racing as she wondered what darkness had borne witness to them. Who—or what—had watched them have sex?

Archer was lying. He had to be. Either that or he'd gone so dark he couldn't even see it. Would a practitioner of black magic think what they were doing was evil? "There was a horrible evil coming from the forest," she insisted now. "Maybe you never saw it coming. Maybe it's what's hurting you now."

He thrust his hand toward the windows of her shop. "The only thing hurting us is those damnable bells. You, who taste of the redbell flower, can you say they aren't what's killing you, too?"

She looked away. She'd answered three of his questions already. She didn't need to tell him more.

"Your protection—whatever cowardly townie thing it is you think you're saving yourself from—is not worth the price we all pay."

Ivy swallowed her words, for they would have been a question. She knew how much her neighbors and their scatterings of forest blood were injured by the bells. How did they torture those in the forest, full-blooded folk like Archer who couldn't move away? She recalled the things he'd shared with his kiss. Sick children, empty huts... *"It must be stopped, or we'll lose them all."*

All these years, she'd listened to the council's dire warnings and worried the forest folk had been wiped out by dark magic. Perhaps they had. Only it wasn't brambles and stone that had defeated them. It was the bells.

What can fight dark magic but more of the same?

And now they had stopped, and he was here. It hurt to breathe. If Archer had turned to dark magic, it was the town what drove him to it.

She looked at her first love again, at the scars crossing his skin, at the defiance in his eyes, at the resentment which poured off him like fever sweat. And she couldn't blame him.

"You still have one more question."

That she did. And now she didn't care about the woman and the children. She only wanted the truth. "What are you doing here?"

He chuckled. "I told you, you don't want to ask me that question."

"Why not?"

"Because, Ivy Potter," he said, and his voice was full of sorrow, "you won't like the answer."

six

"THERE ARE MANY THINGS I DON'T LIKE about this night," Ivy said, as bravely as she could. "But that's my question, and according to your own rules, you're bound to tell me."

Ivy could think of three possibilities, and each one scared her more than the last. Perhaps he was escaping, since the evil in the forest had grown so dangerous that *no one* could withstand it, no matter what dark arts they practiced. Or maybe his task was to bring down the barrier and let enchantment flood the town.

Option three was the most terrifying of all. Maybe he had come for her at last. There were times, especially that first year when her father was still alive and the barrier was making her sick, that she used to dream of it. To imagine Archer breaking the barrier and coming for her. She'd picture him scaling the sheer sides of the gorge or digging tunnels below the earth or bringing down the barrier, bell by wretched bell, to gather her in his arms and tell her that nothing— not dark magic or the town's disapproval, would ever keep them apart.

Those dreams died slowly years ago, worn to tatters by loss and illness and the neverending din of the bells.

Ivy didn't speak again, and she didn't back down. These were the rules of the game.

Archer relented, his shoulders slumping. "We need your father's help. The redbells in the forest are dying out. You must know what that means for us."

She did. Without the flower, they'd never survive the bells' effects. "But my father's gone."

He nodded. "And you run his shop now."

Archer's plan came crashing into view. He'd come for her father, to save the redbells. But her father was dead, and the tea was Ivy's invention.

That meant he *had* come for her.

Once, it would have been all she wanted. To live with Archer in the forest, to be young and free and wild in a place filled with love and enchantment. But Ivy knew better now. She knew the truth of the dangers that the forest held, she knew her place in the modern world, and she knew, most of all, that Archer was not hers. There was that girl in his mind. There were those children. There were the years between them, and most of all, there was the darkness he'd allowed into his heart.

But tonight, the bells had stopped, and in the muffled, snowy stillness, she could hear him breathe, in and out as he watched her, not even blinking. She could hear the tiny voice she'd been ignoring for years as she repeated her father's mantra of safety and security and a small, lonely life. The one that cried out

51

for Archer and adventure and hope and love. It rose within her like a plant in spring sun, a frail shoot with the soul of a forest tree.

She squeezed her eyes shut, willing it to go away. Her father's words echoed in her mind. *You cannot trust forest folk. They don't think as normal people do. They don't want what normal people want. Look at your mother. She loved us and still she left us. Look at every half-blood in this town. The forest lives in their hearts, and their magic will ensnare you, as harmless as it seems.*

Hadn't she seen enough to prove that when the forest folk claimed they'd rather die than leave their villages when the barrier went up? Now here they were — dying, breaking the barrier after all. Here was Archer, filled with dark magic and finally remembering she existed.

You cannot trust forest folk. No matter what he'd once been to her, he could not show up in the middle of the night, suffused with dark magic and dripping with blood, and expect her to trust him. Ivy stepped back.

"Don't run, Ivy." It was almost a sigh. So soft, so final.

"I can't. You've already proven that."

He blinked. He'd not been expecting this response. Not after their little game.

She had to find out the details of his plan. She may not be able to run, but she wasn't going to walk into the forest a willing captive. "Three questions won't do it for me, Archer. Not with what you're proposing."

"I'm not… proposing." Was that a blush stealing across his cheekbones? Whatever it was, it was gone in a flash, replaced by something unreadable and intense. "I'm telling. We need your help in the forest."

"Then you can afford to explain yourself fully. What exactly you want." Her botanical knowledge? Or her, body and soul?

Not that she'd consider that one. It would just be interesting to know, a balm to soothe the devilish parts of her mind.

He hesitated, and there was a world inside his silence. "If I tell you everything, you will use it against me."

Archer always had been able to read her like the tracks in the snow. Once, she'd thought it had been due to that "shared soul" he told her they had. But it was a trick. All just a forest trick. It would be madness to walk into the forest with him now, a repudiation of everything her father had helped her to see when the barrier went up. The forest was dangerous, and Archer was a forest man. Helping him was one thing, but trusting him another.

"Your plan is foolish," she tried. "You don't need my help with the redbells in your cursed woods. You brought the barrier down. Why don't you take your people and escape?"

He looked at her as if she spoke gibberish. "Escape? You have lived across from these bells for years, though I know it must make you as sick as it makes me. Why do you not *escape*?"

She folded her arms. "That's different." But when she went to explain why, her arguments seemed hollow as straw. This was her home—but the forest was home to the folk who dwelt there, too.

Still, her home was real. Safe. Brick and plumbing and roof tar and wires. Not some backward forest hovel. "No one here is dying," she said at last.

"We are only dying because you're killing us," he replied. "We will not abandon our home just because your kind seeks to destroy it."

"We're not destroying anything," she replied. "Just trying to protect ourselves."

"Oh?" he asked wryly. "How safe are you tonight?"

Ivy's breath caught in her throat again, but Archer's expression smoothed and he ran his hand through his hair in frustration.

"I'm wasting precious time. Your townies could discover what I've done any minute. Ivy, I don't wish to make an enemy of you."

"You have a funny way of showing it."

"Please, do not judge me by my behavior this night. To bring down the barrier—" He sighed. "It took a lot out of me. I'm not fully myself."

"Oh, is that what you call it?" she snapped. "You aren't being cranky, Archer. You as good as told me you'd sold your soul."

She expected him to respond, to deny, but he said nothing at all, just stared at her, wistful and sad, and then finally spoke. "This is the truth: we need your help."

How could she trust that? She gave a small shake of her head. "I can't…"

He made as if to close the distance between them, then checked himself. "I don't know how you have managed to keep enough redbell growing in your little greenhouse to see to the needs of your forest-blooded townies, but you have. Meanwhile, we've stripped the forest of nearly all the bulbs. Without them, every person in my village will be dead within the month, thanks to the abomination of your barrier bells."

When Ivy moved this time, it was to sit on the couch. Archer was poised to spring on her again, but stopped as she leaned back on the cushions, as calmly as she could in such a situation. He was still shirtless, he was still standing over her, and he was still threatening to drag her into the woods.

She averted her eyes and kept her tone as cool and logical as she could. "How do you use the plant?"

He narrowed his eyes and lowered himself to the arm of the sofa. Still between her and the door, but like this, she could almost imagine him any normal customer—well, if Ivy had been in the habit of catering to twenty-one-year-old ex-lovers who didn't wear shirts, that was.

"A sliver of redbell bulb beneath the tongue," he said.

She shook her head again. No wonder they were running out. "We make a tea. I can give you the formula—it uses less of the bulb, more of the flowers and the petals. It preserves the bulb for multiple sproutings—"

"No," he replied. "That won't help us. Our redbells are still dying. We don't have enough anymore, even if we did start making tea. They're only found deep in the forest now—far from the sound of your bells. I'm sure I don't have to tell you how dangerous that makes them to harvest."

She shuddered.

"We used to send children to gather them. Now only trained rangers are allowed." He leaned in. "Yet

55

you grow them here? In a town? In full range of the bells? Tell me your secret, Ivy Potter."

She nodded in understanding. This would save her, and take Archer away again. Forever.

"I will show you."

~

George Potter's greenhouse was a marvel. A dome of glass panels, banded and veined by bars of copper and bronze, the better to protect the forest life found within from the poison of modern iron. Everywhere green vines grew, stretching tendrils up toward the sunlight so that during the day, the greenhouse looked less like a building of glass and more like a living bower.

An ivy bower.

Long ago, George Potter had built it with help from a forest girl he'd met while studying the unusual species found inside the unexplored canyon forest. They'd fallen in love—so in love, apparently, that the girl had left the forest to start a family with the young botanist right there in town. Or, at least that's the story he liked to tell.

But by the time their daughter, Ivy, was old enough to remember, her forest-born mother was gone. The greenhouse remained, and so did the botanist, his love for forest plants undiminished by the betrayal he'd suffered at the hands of a forest-dweller.

Ivy knew that most greenhouses didn't look like theirs. She'd seen them on trips she'd taken with her father to the big cities, to academic research labs and garden centers where the plants sat in boxes in neat little rows. She'd found them mystifying, sterile. She'd asked her father how the researchers could study life, with plants that were so thoroughly captive. But their forest's plants, her father had explained, were like the forest folk: impossible to tame, hard to even keep contained. The Potter greenhouse was a maze, a jungle of twisted walkways and overgrown root systems. Some of the plants dwelt in clay pots, true, but most drew their strength from the bare soil beneath the glass.

It was to this greenhouse that Ivy led Archer now, after first giving him a spare shirt that had once belonged to her father. She'd had quite enough of averting her eyes from his well-muscled chest and abs for one evening.

And if her ploy worked, she'd never be troubled by visions of his body again. Her teenaged dreams of running away to live with her boyfriend in an enchanted forest were one thing. Getting dragged into a dying forest and trapped there by a married dark magic practitioner she used to love was quite another.

She just had to keep telling herself that.

The still, snowy night they stepped out into was unbroken by the sound of jangling bells, by the buzz of their power—the power Archer claimed was black magic. Ivy had donned a red fleece sweater over her shirt in deference to the frigid evening. Archer had refused so much as a scarf over the old, plaid shirt she'd given him. Indeed, he'd barely buttoned it, as if even the idea of their modern, machine-stitched clothes with their plastic buttons and factory tags were anathema to him.

It was odd, shuffling across the snow to the backyard greenhouse. Quiet. Ivy had quite forgotten the squeak your boots made against fresh-fallen snow, the tinkle of ice crystals against pine needles. Moonlight sparkled blue and silver on the ground and across the panes of glass that curved above them as they reached the greenhouse door.

She unlocked it and gestured for him to get inside, before the warmth escaped.

"Oh, no, Ivy Potter," he said, and waved his hand. "Ladies first."

She rolled her eyes and entered and he followed close behind. She shut the door. He stilled, like a buck when it hears the snap of a twig or catches the scent of a predator on the wind.

"What's that?" he asked. He was cocking his head, listening. But Ivy knew it would do him little good.

"It's nothing," she replied. "*That's* our secret."

seven

ORIGINALLY, HER PARENTS' PLAN had been to shield the forest plants from the town, from the sounds of motorcars and air conditioners, the buzz of electrical wires, and the smell of diesel and Freon and paint. It had been Ivy's mother's idea to make the greenhouse soundproof, or nearly so. She didn't like the sounds of civilization, so she was sure forest plants wouldn't either.

And once the barrier went up, and the plants nearby died, but the greenhouse flourished, Ivy and her father knew exactly why.

The forest here lived. *Thrived.* All day, all night, every summer and winter. The plants were lush, huge, as only plants who hadn't felt a winter's chill in twenty years could be. Their long, artificial summer benefitted from the soil and the sun that fed this magical slice of Earth, yet were protected from the harsher elements, as well as from the artifices man had brought to this place.

Archer's eyes were wide as he looked around him. This wasn't his first time in their greenhouse, of course. He'd spent many hours wandering its paths with Ivy when he was younger. But memories faded, and the world around them had changed. As a child of the forest, Archer was probably unimpressed with their meager specimens back then, probably hardly noticed the way one couldn't hear street traffic or the quarry shift whistle. Now though, when silence was a golden gift and the forest was withering away behind the barrier...

He closed his eyes and breathed. "It's clean here," he whispered. "Quiet. It's...right."

Ivy knew exactly what he meant. She used to come here, once the forest was cut off but before she'd perfected her tea. She used to lie in the earth and bury herself in leaves and breathe the greenery and remember Archer and the way things used to be. Even now, she loved it here. Loved what it reminded her of—the endless forest of her youth, the enduring proof of the connection her parents must have once shared. Her mom may have gone back to her forest roots, but she'd left plenty here for the Potters.

"See?" she replied. "Plants *can* grow in a cage."

Archer turned to her, eyes blazing. "Then this was your father's plan? Kill the forest and keep his own plants safe?"

"No!" she cried. His words were needles, his glares were knives. "He had no plan." Wasn't the barrier sickness and the loss of their business proof enough of that? "He was only trying to keep the town safe."

In the final days before the barrier went up, when the town buzzed with stories of bramble-men walking out of the trees and infants being replaced with babes of mud, Ivy had expected her father to stand up for the forest, to take a stand against the barrier plans. But he did not.

"The forest teems with evil," he'd said, at a meeting in the center of town, while Ivy sat in her seat in the front row, skin crawling at the accusing eyes around her, head tucked down against her chest as she'd heard the attacks against the forest folk she'd loved. "I've explored its depths and I know what I've seen. Though my livelihood comes from the forest, though my own daughter is half forest blood" —here he pointed at Ivy, and she heard the rumblings through the audience— "I can no longer ignore its dangers. We must put up the barrier. It's the only thing that will protect our families. Protect us all."

It was then that Ivy knew the barrier would be raised. If even her father was an advocate, then the town was joined in agreement. There was no other way.

"It was luck alone that the greenhouse saved these plants," she said to Archer now. "We didn't know the forest would be hurt by the bells. We didn't know *we* would. We were just trying to protect ourselves from the wave of dark magic coming our way."

"There was no wave of dark magic," he said, his tone filled with disbelief and contempt. "If the forest is darker than it used to be—if *we* are— it's from desperation. It's rot."

"That can't be." She shook her head wildly. "Maybe the very presence of the bells stopped it, even for your side. Maybe it drove the darkness back into the depths, and it never came at all. But it *was* coming.

61

We'd already seen the first wave." Her father had, at least. "Changelings and demon men... and worse things yet. Things my father wouldn't even tell me, back then. We had to protect ourselves or we'd have been destroyed. That forest teems with evil."

"How would you know?" he snapped back at her. "Hiding here—in your iron-choked town. In your silent, safe greenhouse." He jabbed his finger against his own chest. "*I'm* the one who knows every twig of that forest. I'm the one who has lived there, who has watched people run mad or wither away when they have no choice, who has watched children die— not because of any dark forest magic, but because of *your* curse."

And now she, too, had seen those dying children. Maybe Archer's children. That had never been their intent—the council who'd erected the barrier. They'd been trying to *protect* the town's children, to protect everyone. That's what her father said.

"And what of your curses, Archer?" she asked him. "You've admitted to me that you've been doing dark magic. What horrible acts have you committed to make sure my entire town is now in danger from your precious forest?"

His eyes narrowed. "Every word from your mouth is a lie, Ivy Potter. But I no longer know which ones you yourself believe." Archer turned from her now and walked a few steps down the path, his back straight and proud as he passed beneath the boughs. His left hand drifted outward to trace the whorls of gnarled bark on one trunk. He stopped, reached farther. His shoulders lifted.

In the stillness, Ivy could swear she heard him breathe.

Memories crowded in on all sides, twining through her mind like insistent vines. The feel of his chest moving beneath her head as they rested, wrapped around each other in the treetops. The taste of his tongue in the morning, when books and TV shows told her it should have been gross, but always tasted to her just like Archer. She could have kissed him any time in the day or night. There was a time when she thought she'd hear his breath in her ear every morning for eternity.

Her mouth still tingled from where he'd kissed her, her body from where he'd wrapped his arms around her and held tight. Her entire palm felt on fire. She couldn't believe she'd grabbed his balls. What difference did it make, really? She hadn't taken the opportunity to escape.

The second she'd touched him she'd almost forgotten why she needed to run at all. Right now, she couldn't remember her mantras, her need for safety, her decision to send him away.

He stood, as still as a deer, beneath the branching tree by the side of the path, half turned away from her, as though he'd forgotten she was there. She soaked in every detail—the way his hair curled over his collar, how he held his arms out slightly from his side, as if the shirt bothered him, the way the light dappled through the leaves and onto his winter-pale skin.

He was so beautiful. And so very, very far away.

In the green and golden stillness of this place, she could almost see it, shimmering at his edges like violet-black mirage. Whatever wretched enchantment had made his eyes turn black, it still lay upon him, a cloak of dark magic enshrouding his soul. She wondered what it might look like to someone who actually could do magic, to Archer, or that forest woman from his memories. A suit of snakes, perhaps, or bramble vines.

Did it disgust him? Would it disgust her, if she could see it clearly?

Who was she kidding? Ivy had been admiring his naked chest even as she washed blood from his skin. She'd been distracted by the sight of his forest-hewn body even as she questioned whether he was still Archer inside. The gossip she'd endured in high school may have faded, but it was as true now as it was then. There was no mistaking Ivy's twisted, forest-lover tastes. Even bristling with dark magic, Archer made her ache.

Had the barrier never been placed, she would have ended up a woman like the ones in the posters, wasting away in the forest or stuck in town with forest-blooded babies after her lover abandoned her for the wild.

Babies. That possibility had seemed eons away to her as a teenager, but the glimpse she'd seen into Archer's memories had been anything but.

"The children," she blurted before she lost her nerve. "The woman. In your mind. Are they... yours?"

If possible, his back went even straighter. "Yes."

She was glad he wasn't facing her now, as she couldn't hide the anguish that overcame her at the words. Of course they were. *Of course*. He was a forest man. They didn't wait long—there was no college to think of first. He had met another girl, made babies— babies that should have been hers.

Ivy sucked in a breath and blinked away the moisture stinging her eyes. Why cry now? Archer had been lost to her three years ago. That future could never come to pass. But thinking it was one thing— seeing his children, his woman, hearing confirmation that he'd moved on... That was something else.

But hers or not, she would not let Archer's children die. She couldn't follow him into the forest, but she could still help his family.

She fought to draw breath enough to speak. "This way to the redbells," she choked out, and slid past him on the path. *Don't touch, don't look. He's not yours.* "I'll give you a large supply of tea and my parents' plans for the greenhouse. The tea will sustain you while you build your own..."

"Build?" he sneered. "Because there is such a supply of glass and bronze in the forest?"

"Oh." Ivy flinched. She hadn't even thought of that. And they wouldn't have the craftsmen or carpenters either. But that couldn't be her problem. "That's all I can offer you. That's what makes the plants grow. There's no other secret. There's nothing my going back with you can accomplish. I can give you tea; I can give you redbells. The rest is up to you." She dared to look over her shoulder at him, but his expression was unreadable. "Please, Archer. I'm telling you the truth. There is no other secret. There's nothing else I can do for you."

"No," he said softly. "There never was, was there?"

"And let's be honest — what would you do with me, back in your forest?" She forced a laugh. "I am, as you say, a townie."

"Yes," he repeated, his voice flat. "You're a townie."

Maybe that's what they both needed. To say these things over and over, loud enough to drown out the tiny drumbeat in her head that said *him him him him him*.

She led the way to the plot of redbells, tucked away beneath the spreading branches of a forest willow up near the far end of the dome, where the hot air of the greenhouse met the glass in smears of condensation against the window. Beyond the panes, the forest spread out, black and silent. Silent as it hadn't been for years.

"Here they are." She knelt in the flowers and took a bloom in the palm of her hand. He crouched beside her, closer than she would have liked. It was warm here, but heat still poured off him in waves, and she had to clench her muscles to keep from leaning into it, from leaning into him. She could hear him breathe, and she knew, she just knew if she touched him she could hear everything else besides.

"You can have half the crop," she said, instead of all of the things she wanted to. "And most of my tea supply." She'd have enough for her clients until she rebuilt. She'd give him everything she could, if it would save his children, and the others from the forest village. "You can take it all. You don't need me."

"No," he agreed, and cupped a redbell blossom. "I don't need—" But his words cut off as the flower withered and blackened in his hand. Hissing, Archer dropped the burnt flower to the ground and stood.

Ivy looked at him in shock. "What did you do?"

eight

ARCHER JERKED HIS HEAD AND LOOKED AWAY. "It's nothing. It'll fade."

"But what happened?" Ivy went on, staring at the destroyed redbell in horror and disgust "Is it from coming through the barrier?"

"In a manner of speaking."

She nodded in understanding. "It's the magic, isn't it? Whatever dark rites you performed to silence the bells. It still courses in you."

Still looking away, he replied. "Yes. But like I said, it'll fade. Though I shouldn't touch your crop until it does." He picked up the wilted flower again. The blackened edges burned and crumpled until nothing remained but a handful of ashes. He clapped his palms, and then the ashes, too, vanished.

A shiver stole across Ivy's skin, a whisper of darkness, like she, too, could scorch if she dared to get any closer to Archer. "When? When will it fade?"

He stared down at the smear of dirt still blackening his hands. "I don't know." He was silent for a long moment. "It'll fade. It has to."

"You don't know?" she blurted. What had he done so dark that he had no idea when the curse would leave him?

"No." Archer still stared into the plot of flowers, his jaw set, his eyes distant. And then, abruptly, he plopped back on the ground, sitting beside her and pressing his forehead to his knees. "No one has ever done this before. No one has ever made it through the barrier and survived."

Her hand hovered over his shoulder, afraid to touch, as if she too would blacken and blow away. He looked at once like the boy she'd known. No longer terrifying, no longer *other*. He looked young. Scared. "Archer…"

"What you do is, you start small," he said into the ground. "Little rites, tiny curses. They curdle your heart, but I had no choice. You have to build up to the type of darkness what can kill the bells. That's where the others went wrong, I thought. They went too dark, all at once."

"The others," Ivy murmured, half to herself.

"Every solstice for three years." He raised his head and looked at her. "The things I did—I sacrificed animals, I cast curses. I didn't want to— I couldn't bear to hurt others, so I cast them on myself. It was the only way. Curses of pain and anger and despair."

Are you Archer, or are you some dreadful thing made to look like him?

I ask myself that every day.

Since he'd awoken, brimming with dark magic, she'd allowed herself to believe horrible things, to picture blood-soaked rites or unspeakable deeds. But somehow knowing the truth was even worse, that Archer—her sweet, loving Archer—had been so unwilling to let others suffer for the power he hoped to gain that he cursed himself. She remembered the new scars on his skin, recalled the angry words he'd thrown at her and the sadness that filled his face when he spoke about the past.

What memories, what dreams had he sacrificed to bring down the bells?

"I thought I was going to die tonight, like the others did. When I woke up and you were standing over me, your hair all white and glowing in the firelight—" He reached out and stroked her cheek with the back of his hand. It tingled against her skin, but did not burn. "You looked like an angel, Ivy. I wondered if I was dead after all." He leaned in.

Ivy shot up and strode into the flowers, the scent of redbell filling her head and hopefully driving away whatever dark magic Archer wove with his words. Forest tricks, forest tricks. She was always such a sucker for them. Ivy didn't stop until she reached the glass, and she rested her cheek against the frozen pane, icing away the memory of Archer's touch.

"Hoped I was, even," he called after her, his voice booming through the greenhouse like wishing for death was something to admit out loud. "I didn't like the person I was becoming, all these months. All this dark magic. I don't love the memory of the things I did to get here, of the sacrifices I've made."

She should send him away. Home to his forest woman and his sick children. They could wrap her redbells in packs of greenhouse moss — it should protect them from whatever curse lay upon her old lover, at least for long enough for him to bring the life-saving flowers back to his home.

"Ivy." The whisper felt close enough to come from inside her own head. Her eyes flew open and met Archer's. He stood half a pane of glass away, leaning against the outer wall as if for support. "Don't you see? It was all worth it, to be here with you." He touched her again, and a vision bloomed in her head—the perfect summer night where they'd given themselves to one another beneath a fat, white moon.

She pulled back. "Don't you dare." That memory was hers to savor, not his to manipulate. Hers to keep and cherish, no matter what else had followed. Losing him, her father, losing everyone, the bells, those bells, those awful years of bells. And tonight, worst of all, with the bells gone and Archer here and knowing he still wasn't hers, could never be hers. Magic or no, bells or silence, Archer was forest and she was town and that was the way it was.

"I thought I'd die tonight," he said. "Die without ever seeing you again. I thought I'd convinced myself that I didn't care, that you were just some townie who'd abandoned me."

"Abandoned *you*?" she whispered, as angrily as she could whisper. He'd never know what she went through the night the barrier went up.

"You were my first great curse, you see. Trapped away in the forest, my love for you was a flower caught in amber, ever safe."

She sealed her lips over the choking, little cry that erupted from her throat. That couldn't be true. What about the woman? The children?

"Until last year, when I knew it would have to be me to take on the bells this solstice. I killed animals, burnt living trees. I cast curses on myself, spells of sorrow and rage. I left the village, was shunned by the others…"

Unbidden, the image of Archer wreathed in firelight loomed up in her mind's eye. Laughing, lighthearted Archer, who loved chocolate and tree-climbing and being kissed in the hollow of his throat. The forest folk must have been desperate indeed, to turn to him to save them.

"By the equinox, I was ready, and I knew which curse to choose." He reached for her, his fingers hooking round a curl of her blonde hair. "You were a golden gem, hidden away in my heart, but I had the tools to smash you into shards. It gave me power; to hate you, Ivy Potter, it made me strong." He released the strand of her hair and stared down at his ashen hands. "But it made me hideous, too. It's a wonder you can't see it. There has been none but forest folk to lay eyes on me until tonight, and they never did it unless they had to. I came to think I was as ugly as I appeared, until…"

Until she looked at him. Ivy and her unmagical eyes. How silly, to think that it was the Archer free of glamour who was the more beautiful. But she supposed it made sense. After all, the enchantments he wore were reflections of the darkness in his soul. To forest folk, the fact that she couldn't see how horrible he'd become within was the fault, his skin-deep beauty the disguise.

The darkness buzzed around him like angry gnats, and she was sure that if she were magic, he'd look terrifying indeed. "You did look scary to me," she admitted. "When you first woke up. Your eyes were black, all black, like a frog or a spider's eyes."

He blinked at her, his eyebrows arching over green eyes wide with surprise. "And they aren't now?"

She shook her head. "No. For a while, in the shop, they changed back and forth, but—" She shrugged. "It's just traces of my forest blood. Don't mind me."

"I always mind you."

Now, she shut her eyes, squeezed them tight, because it was her only choice. Her ears, sensitized to silence after years of the barrier din, thrilled at every syllable. She couldn't shut him out, his soft, whispered words. No matter how much she wanted to, needed to, in order to keep to the path she'd started down all those years ago.

She replayed the night in her mind, trying to make sense of it all. "When you first woke up," she said, eyes still closed, "you looked wrong. But then, after you..." She took a deep, shuddering breath. "After you kissed me, I thought it must have been a mistake, because your eyes were green again."

"And they stayed green."

She opened her eyes to find him staring at her intently. "No. They... they flickered for a while." She tried to back away, to find the curve of the glass against her back. "What does it matter, Archer? Must you know *exactly* how blind I am to your forest enchantments?"

He contemplated her. "You are not blind—not exactly. To someone like me, you are nearsighted. You only see the greatest, most blatant of magics. Perhaps the curse that enveloped me when I attacked the bells is already fading."

She glanced out the window at the silent forest. "Does that mean they will start to ring again?" There was a catch in her voice that betrayed her, though she wasn't sure of its cause. Did she fear that Archer would be trapped here with her, or that he'd be unable to carry her off?

Impossible options, both.

"No," he said. "The spell is broken. The forest is free… for now."

Meaning until the townsfolk chose to the raise the barrier again, of which Ivy held little doubt. A wild, wicked, bloody forest man who broke through at midnight and freely boasted of the dark magic he'd wrought to thwart them? They as good as had a new face for their posters.

"The forest is free," she repeated, "but you are cursed."

"Yes," he whispered. "More's the pity for those I force into my company."

Her gaze shot back to him, her mouth a thin line. "I will not go with you. You can have my flowers, nothing more."

Archer pressed closer, trapping her between the glass and the planes of his chest. "I will have what I say."

His voice made her weak; her body quaked with desire. But it was impossibly wrong to listen, to even so much as imagine. Ivy swallowed, tilting her chin up to give him a fearful glance. "Please. I cannot help you by going with you. Just take my redbells and leave."

"And I cannot bear to leave you here." The words tore out of him. "Don't you see? I cannot even curse you away, Ivy. I tried, and it is clear to me I

73

failed. All the blood and sacrifice, and the dread I cast upon my soul... do you know what the darkest wish in my heart is right now?"

The moment stretched out like eternity. Ivy didn't want to know.

But Archer spoke anyway. "I would trample your entire crop if it meant I had an excuse to haul you back into the forest and keep you there forever."

She shoved at his shoulders, panic overtaking all her good sense to avoid his touch. "I will not! Go away, Archer. Go home. You have a wife, you have *children.*"

He stared at her for a second, confused, and then his expression softened. For a second, she thought he might laugh.

"What?" she asked, appalled. She stopped shoving, but her palms remained on his chest.

"Nephews," he replied, leaning in. "And the girl I guess you saw was my brother's."

Her eyes narrowed. "You said they were yours!"

"They are. My responsibility, I mean. Everything I've done, it's for them. My brother's dead. He was the last to attempt the solstice rites."

Ivy vaguely remembered Archer's older brother. Solemn and serious where her lover had been bright and charming. Like Ivy's own mother, he'd been a ranger long before Ivy and Archer had gone from childhood friends to something more, and she'd only met him a handful of times.

And now Ivy knew they both had lost someone at the barrier. But then why had Archer made her think the children were his? "Forest tricks," she mumbled. She had to remember. "Forest tricks."

"I do not lie, Ivy. You know that. The children you saw in my vision… how old are they?"

Ivy blinked. That was a good point. She wasn't good with estimating the age of kids. There were so few in this neighborhood, after all. But the ones she'd seen in Archer's memories weren't babies. And they would have to be, wouldn't they? Three years wasn't enough for Archer to have anything older than a toddler, even if he'd started right away.

Forest tricks, indeed. No wonder he was laughing at her mistake.

"But they are still my responsibility," he said. "I cannot leave them to their fate in the forest."

What would his responsibility have been to children he left in town? Her mother hadn't seemed to mind leaving Ivy there. Forest folk weren't very consistent when it came to such things. "And what would have happened to them had you died during your ritual tonight?"

"I would have died trying to save them," he pointed out. "As my brother did. That's different."

She didn't need to hear his forest folk logic. Dead was dead, and alone was alone, no matter what lofty ideals had preceded the action. It didn't matter if her father had been despairing of the loss of the forest, or reaching for a flower, or if he'd just tripped and fallen into the barrier. He was gone, either way.

"You liked making me think they were yours," Ivy accused Archer. "Admit it."

"Fine." His jaw was set. "I was less than forthcoming. Does it make you happy I'm still bitter you chose your precious town over me?"

"You chose the forest over me!" she snapped at him. "You could have left back then. My father warned you all—"

"More lies!" he replied. "And you accuse me of trickery, of treachery? Your father told us *nothing*. We had no idea we were about to be trapped. Remember how I said I came looking for you the day after the bells began to ring? Would I have done so if I'd known there was no way across the barrier?"

Ivy felt like she might choke. Her arms dropped to her sides. Her father had told everyone he'd gone to the forest people and presented his case. Why would he lie? She remembered how heartbroken he'd been that they rejected him. He'd told her how they'd laughed at him, rebuffed him, called him a silly townie. He'd explained how even his wife—even Ivy's mother—had chosen the forest over her own safety.

He'd told her all of this, and Ivy had comforted him. It *had* to be true. The life she'd lived, the duties she'd upheld, the torture she'd suffered and the feelings she was even now at this moment fighting to deny—it had to be true. The forest was evil, the folk there were fickle, the town was safe, and her choices were right.

Archer leaned in now, his hands braced above her on the thick, wavy glass. "Don't you think if he'd warned us, I would have run to town to be with you? Ivy, Ivy, did you think so little of me as to believe that?"

She swallowed, hard, the council's posters flashing before her eyes. The vine-wrapped girl sentenced to a life of forest drudgery, the men with eyes of violets, the roar of rumors in town warning of

76

forest men and forest tricks. The words of her father, echoing in her head every day and night as she tried to convince herself he was right. *The forest folk are different. The forest folk cannot be trusted. They don't think as we do, don't live as we do, can't love as we do…*

"I would have given up everything I'd ever known to be with you," he cried. "But you… you, who knew the barrier would go up, did *you* come for me?"

Ivy hung her head, miserable. That awful night. She hadn't even heard the bells start to ring, she'd been so encased in her own despair. This was the problem with having a boyfriend who had no email, no cell phone, not even a real address. She couldn't tell him that even as his cage lowered, she was trapped, too.

"I tried."

"What?" It was more a breath than a word. She couldn't face him, though he was only inches away.

"I tried, Archer. I would have given it all up, too. My father had to lock me in my room the night the bells began to ring."

Silence fell, a quiet more complete than a snowy night, unbroken by the jangle of silver bells. Blood rushed in Ivy's ears, her heart pounded, but she didn't breathe. Neither did Archer.

Instead, he wrapped his arms around her and three years of waiting crashed down around them both.

nine

THIS ONE COULDN'T PROPERLY BE CALLED a
kiss either. Kisses were gentle, sweet. Kisses were
things given on altars when you wore white lace and
flowers. Kisses belonged to babies and friends and
shy boys on first dates. This was mouths and breath
and wanting so bad it might singe off their skin. This
was hands clutching and nails scraping and clothes
rent at the seams.

"Ivy," he said or breathed or thought directly
into her soul. She couldn't tell. She didn't care. "Ivy-
mine."

"Yes," she gasped, though pausing for breath
seemed so beyond the point. "Yours."

The old plaid shirt went flying, and her sweater
seemed to shred like fine silk. Maybe it was magic,
maybe even dark magic, but Ivy barely noticed. She
was too busy taking stock of every square inch of her
skin that touched his skin, and thinking it was a
miracle. Everything else about this night—the bells,

the arguments, the threats—nothing else mattered. This was Archer, here, for her. This was the thing she'd told herself she didn't want, couldn't have, mustn't crave. Ivy no longer cared.

"Bras?" he grumbled, his face buried in her collarbone. "I forgot how much I hated bras. You want dark magic? Whoever invented these things should be cursed."

"Mmmm," Ivy replied, and unhooked hers. She flung the cups away, and they landed on a bush halfway down the greenhouse walk. "Better?"

"Partly." He glared at her jeans. "You've already seen me without my pants."

She kicked off her boots, undid her jeans, then shoved them down too. "Now better?"

"Panties," he said, smiling. "Not like bras. So much better than bras." He hooked his fingers into the scraps of cotton fabric at her hips. "What happened to all those lace and bows and strings you used to wear?"

"It's been three years since anyone's seen them, Archer. Lace and bows are itchy."

He fell against her, burning Archer on her front, the frozen glass at her back. "Ivy," he groaned in wonder. "No one…?"

"I told you." She pressed herself into his embrace, moaning. "I'm yours."

And she was. They'd played games and they'd tossed about anger and accusations and yes, even lies, but they couldn't deny it. He was hers and she was his and they had the same soul. Didn't they know that? Didn't everyone know? Her father had locked her away, the town had put up a wall of magic between them, but here they were again.

His beard scraped the skin of her face, her throat. This beard that he hadn't had when they'd been teenagers but still felt as familiar as her own hand. His palms covered her breasts, hot and gentle, possessive and perfect. She whimpered when his thumbs grazed her nipples and his tongue delved into her belly button, she writhed when his hands slipped down to divest her of her underwear, she bit her lip over a scream when she felt him nuzzling her thighs apart.

Before she could stop him, he'd hooked one of her legs over his shoulder and his mouth moved against areas of her body that hadn't felt the touch of anything but her own fingers in ages. And this wasn't kissing either, exactly, but my oh my, she was fine with it, too.

More than fine. Way, way, way more than fine. Her hands glided over the steam-soaked panes of the glass, searching for something to grip. When she found nothing, she reached for him, swept her fingers through his mass of curls, threw her head back, and gave into the sensations he was sending through her with his lips and tongue and voice rumbling her name in a tone almost too low to hear.

Her nerve endings blazed and her mind was filled with memories of summer nights, the taste of creekwater and woodwine and salt from Archer's skin, the evenings she thought she could live on nothing but sex and forest magic, and she didn't care what the kids at school would say Monday morning, when her locker would be filled with leaves and pebbles, and her father would shake his head and tell her to be careful, be careful, be oh so very—

Archer's tongue pressed against her flesh just so and Ivy cried out, shuddering in sudden, shattering pleasure, half here and half in the memories they both shared. If this was magic, then so be it. Ivy would cross her heart and hope to die and let Archer turn her to stone or smoke or rain. As long as she could feel this way for one more moment.

He rose before her, that wild look in his eyes. The one she was supposed to fear. But all she did was want it, and when she kissed him this time, it was a real kiss, full lips and breath and the tang of her pleasure on his tongue. She licked his bottom lip, and nibbled, and smiled against his mouth.

"I'm getting cold, Archer," she begged him coyly. "Make me warm." She rubbed her body against his. He was so hot. Hot like a rock in the summer sun. She wanted to spread herself over him and soak him up.

"Wait, Ivy," he mumbled, fiddling with the fastenings on his own pants. "Wait, Ivy, I have to—"

She lowered her mouth to the hollow of his throat and bit, then quickly laved the spot with her tongue. The nice spot, the one he liked, had always liked. The one she knew because he was always hers.

And just as she wanted, Archer groaned and squeezed his eyes shut as she reached into his pants and took him in her hands. They fell against the glass. Steam rose around them, wafting through her hair and over her feverish skin. She felt his fingers between her legs, felt one slide slick inside her, testing.

"Three years," she reminded him, and pulled him in for a kiss. "Don't make me wait another second."

Archer didn't. He gathered her close, lifting her easily as she wrapped her legs around him. His pants still hung low around his hips, the waistband rubbing against the underside of her thighs. She felt him push inside her, the hard, hungry warmth of Archer filling her up. Ivy breathed out, her sigh swirling the steam that wreathed around them and radiated outward, cloaking this part of the greenhouse dome like a silver curtain. She couldn't see the night or the stars or the snow. She couldn't see anything but Archer.

She fought for leverage as he began to move inside her, pressing her spine against the cool, slippery glass at her back, sliding her hands up the panes to grasp at the metal veins crisscrossing the dome. Her skin squeaked over the glass, chilly water dripping down her shoulder blades in contrast to the fire building between them.

Her head overflowed with memories, Archer's and hers blending, her feelings and thoughts mixing with his until she wasn't sure where she ended and he began. Three years of wanting doubled in her head as she felt his desire and his wonder crashing over and through her.

And yet, how could it be a surprise? How could she ever want anything more than this, than him? She'd worked to deny it, forget it, and why? Nothing could compare to this, this spiral of pleasure, his and hers combined, reflected back and forth in an endless chain.

As soon as Ivy found a grip against the bronze bands, Archer allowed his hands to slip from her back, to grasp her hips and thrust with more force. Steam rose around them, thick and heavy and smelling of trees and earth and a raging fire, the kind that opens pine cones and scares town folk. Ivy didn't want to feel the cold anymore. She just wanted Archer. Even as his ragged, half-formed desires filled her head, she wanted more. Some were fine and beautiful, and some were base and dirty, and she loved them all.

She pulled herself forward and wrapped her arms around his shoulders. He staggered back and lowered himself to the ground, lying down as she straddled him. Ivy pressed down on his chest and moved on top of him, finding a rhythm that worked for them both. His moss-colored eyes stared up at her, smooth and even and filled with an emotion Ivy didn't dare name. Her pale, blonde hair tumbled over her shoulders, and she swiped it out of her face as she leaned down and kissed him again.

His hands tightened on her waist and his hips thrust up, lifting them both off the ground. "Ivy, oh, Ivy…" And then, abruptly, he pulled her off him and gasped, taking his shaft in his hand as his orgasm hit. Ivy nearly cried out too, as the connection between them was severed.

At last he relaxed, his head lolling against the ground as he sighed in pleasure. He reached for her and gathered her close, so her head was tucked into the hollow spot between his collarbone and his chest. She could feel his heart thumping against her temple, strong and fast. His contentment enveloped them both, and as she laid her hand on his chest, she saw herself through his eyes, lifted up against the dome glass, her head thrown back in pleasure. She closed her eyes, suddenly embarrassed, and he squeezed her.

"You all right?"

She nodded against his muscles. "You just surprised me… when you pulled away."

"I wanted to protect you. I didn't know if you still took those pills."

She didn't, and the fact that Archer had thought of that, that he could even remember it when Ivy could hardly remember her own name, amazed her. She pulled herself up and kissed him, long and gentle, running her fingers through the silky strands of his beard for the first time. "This is nice," she said, stroking the bit of hair on his face. It was easier than everything else she wanted to say. "New."

He stretched, smiling. "Yes, well, we can also discuss the changes in your breasts, if you'd like."

She swatted him, and he shifted to avoid her. She heard the crush of plant matter.

"Archer, sit up. You're crushing the redbells."

He pushed himself up on his elbows. "What?"

She pointed at the flowers underneath them. "Get up. You're ruining my crop."

He looked, then let out a whoop of triumph. "I am!"

She crossed her arms over her bare breasts. "Yeah. It's nothing to get excited about."

"Of course it is, Ivy-mine!" he cried, and took her hands in his. All at once, he was the Archer she'd loved as a teen, bright and shining and full of light. "I'm crushing them, not burning them to a crisp. The curse is gone!"

It was true. Whatever remnants of dark magic had lingered in Archer, it seemed to have dissipated. "So what? I…we…" Had the sex somehow fixed him?

"Possibly," he said, as if she'd spoken the thought aloud. "It did feel like magic."

He grinned, but Ivy looked away and reached for her pants. This was a little too much magic for one night. Before, in the heat of the moment, she didn't care, but come morning, there would be lots of questions, and far too few answers. Surely the council would want the bells to ring again. And she and Archer might be fine, this one timeless hour in her greenhouse, but then what? There were too many people in town who feared dark magic, and Archer had family left alone in a dying forest.

She pulled on her panties and jeans, and as she was slipping her feet back into her shoes, another question occurred to her.

Archer said George Potter had never warned them about the creation of the bell barrier, but she'd never forget the look on her father's face when he returned from the forest and said the people there wouldn't leave. It had made perfect sense to Ivy. After all, even now, with barrier sickness and a dying forest, Archer still claimed the forest folk considered it home.

But Archer also said he would have come to be with her, had he known, and Ivy believed him with a bone-deep surety.

So what was the truth?

ten

THE STREET OUTSIDE THE SHOP crawled with townspeople. Up and down the road they walked, examining the silent bells from every angle—every angle, that is, that existed on this side. No one yet had dared try to cross.

Wrapped in bathrobes, Ivy and Archer watched from the attached apartment's bedroom window.

"There's no way you can make it through without them seeing you," Ivy said.

"What do I care?" Archer replied, shrugging. "I'm not trying to keep what I did a secret."

"I care." Ivy tied the knot of her robe more tightly and smoothed her hair. "What do you think they'll do when they find a forest man on this side of the bells?"

"What can they do to me, Ivy?" He spread his hands, curling his fingers in, and the hair on the back of Ivy's neck stood on end. What bloomed there,

86

invisible in his palms? "If they come for me, they will be sorry."

She grabbed his wrist, and got a static shock for her trouble. At least, she hoped it was just static. "No dark magic, Archer. What are you thinking?"

He blinked down at her grip on him. "I don't know," he said, honestly. "These days, I go quickly to curses. Last week, I killed a rabbit just by looking at it."

Ivy winced. She'd heard more than one confession this morning of his time spent with the dark arts. This year had been a lonely, wretched one, and the more powerful he grew, the more even his own folk had rejected him, for their own safety. "That's all over with. The barrier is down now. You won't be doing any more dark magic."

"It's not that simple," he began.

A knock broke the stillness of the shop. It was coming from the front door.

"Well, here's something simple. Stay put and let me do the talking." She headed out into the hall, closing the bedroom door behind her and trying to shake off her unease. If she had anything to say about it, Archer would never practice dark magic again. If she'd been with him in the forest, she'd have never even let him try.

Now she'd found him again, and she wasn't letting go.

Waiting for her on her front porch was the head of the town council, Ernest Beemer, in a long, wool coat and a ridiculous pair of red earmuffs that only emphasized the size of his bald, fat head. Beemer had been one of the ones to first propose the barrier. He owned the quarry, and claimed bramble-men from the forest regularly broke his machinery and poked holes in the dam. His business had boomed since the bells began to ring.

Ivy sighed. She could do this.

"Mr. Beemer?" she asked, as she opened the door. "I'm surprised to see you at my shop. I'm not due to open for another hour…"

"Have you noticed anything, Ivy?"

She raised her eyebrows. "Excuse me?"

"The bells." He gestured to the forest behind him. "Some time in the night, they stopped."

"Really?" She pressed a hand to her chest. "How odd? No, I had no idea. I sleep with this white-noise machine, see, so…"

"And there's a break in the lattice. Right across from your shop." Ernest stepped away and pointed at the hole where she'd found Archer. "It snowed last night, so we haven't been able to find any tracks—"

Thank goodness for small favors, Ivy thought.

"—but the dogs have been sniffing from the break to your door."

"Dogs?" Ivy blurted. "Why, Mr. Beemer, you don't think anything dangerous came from the forest, do you? And cased my little shop? How wretched!" She pulled the lapels of her bathrobe closed, affecting a little shiver. "I'm so glad I invested in that extra padlock. Even if something tried to break in, they wouldn't be able to." There, that ought to do it.

Behind Ernest, on the street, she saw Jeb and Sallie walk by, looking equal parts confused and relieved. They saw her at the door and waved in greeting. She nodded, and turned back to the councilman, who was watching her, brows furrowed. He pulled out a walkie-talkie and spoke into it. "Hey,

Ryder, I'm talking to the Potter girl now. She says she heard nothing, not even the silence."

Must mean Deacon Ryder, another council member. He'd designed every poster that appeared in town while they'd campaigned for the barrier, convinced that forest magic was demonic, and that fighting for the bells meant fighting for the very soul of the town.

And though Ernest walked a few steps away as the reply crackled back, Ivy heard it anyway. "Check around the greenhouse anyway. You know that girl's got forest blood."

She really wished they'd stop calling her a girl. She'd been living alone and running a business for two years now. She wasn't a girl when she paid her bills and worked for her customers. She hadn't been a girl last night when Archer had made her come against the greenhouse dome.

But she wasn't about to point *that* out to the gentlemen from the town council.

"I should probably get dressed," she said brightly to Ernest. "Overslept a bit this morning. Maybe that's the effect of no bells, huh, Mr. Beemer? For the first time in years, we've all gotten a good night's sleep?"

He grunted at her and she shut the door. That was true, at least. She hadn't slept so well in years, though whether it was from the silence or from the fact that she lay in Archer's arms, she didn't know. It was as if she'd fallen through a time warp, and was seventeen again. The wild, cruel Archer who'd awoken on the couch had vanished, leaving nothing behind but cocoa and charm and laughter and kisses. Even if it was all a dream, Ivy wasn't sure she wanted to wake up.

89

Back in her bedroom, Archer was already wearing his forest pants and had found an old sweater somewhere. Ivy was relieved to see him clothed. It would make this easier.

"We need to talk," she said to him. She'd said it last night, too, while they were still half-dressed in the greenhouse, but it hadn't exactly happened. Instead, they'd gotten snacks and settled down in front of the fire to eat, and then they'd jumped all over each other and the only words they'd spoken had been each other's names and cries of pleasure until they'd drifted off into sated sleep some time before dawn.

But now it was daylight, and they really, really needed to talk. About the forest, and the bells, and the scars of dark magic that lay across her lover's soul. The curses might have left him enough to handle her redbell, but Archer wasn't free. Not if he truly had spent months cultivating dark magic in order to break the enchantment on the bells. Magic bore a price.

"Right. Let's talk." He grabbed for her, but she sidestepped him and went behind her closet door.

"You said last night my father never told your people about the bells." She quickly changed out of her robe and into another pair of jeans and a sweater. "And it's not that I don't believe you... I'm just wondering if there could be some kind of mistake." After all, if the forest was overrun with dark magic, maybe her father had walked into some sort of illusion and didn't realize it.

"What sort of mistake?" Archer asked from the other side of the door. "Either he told us or he didn't. And I know he didn't."

She came out, pulling her curls back into a clip. "I mean... maybe there was a forest trick of some kind. Like he thought he was talking to your village but it was enchantment. That can happen."

But Archer looked skeptical. "Of course it can. But your father was experienced in the ways of the forest. He would have seen the signs of an illusion, same as you or I."

In fact, her father had taught her the signs before he'd taught her to ride a bike. Did the images waver, like those seen through water? Did things move and change whenever she blinked? Did she ask them questions only she would know, and they answered as if she asked whether it was night or day? She knew how to tell. It was basic forest safety.

But something had to explain why her father would have made such a terrible error. He died thinking Ivy's mother had turned her back on them for good. It was one thing when she'd gone back to the forest. He seemed to understand it, and they still saw each other. There were plenty of people in the neighborhood, back then, who had forest lovers they saw only once in a while. As a teen, Ivy had even wondered if that's how she and Archer would end up, splitting time between forest and town.

"But what else could it be?"

Archer said nothing, but took her hand. "It doesn't matter now, Ivy. The barrier is down and we are here, together. Those three years are past."

She yanked her hand back. "They aren't! People died. Your entire village is on the brink of destruction. And it wasn't necessary. They could have been saved…"

"Knowing the why will not change the past, Ivy," said Archer. "What good will it do? Trust me, the answer is none."

Ivy brushed past him and out of the room. Down the hall, the door to her father's bedroom lay closed, as always, but she went right in. It was bigger than hers. She probably should have packed his things up long ago and cleaned it out, but she hadn't. She hadn't done any of the things she should have—defy her father, ask unlikely questions, wonder why even her mother, even Archer, would not have railed against being separated from her forever...

She'd believed everyone, and she did what they told her, and she stayed inside and she brewed tea and she let them box her in, bells or no bells. Ivy was tired of playing by the rules.

She yanked open his dresser drawers. "Maybe there's an answer in here somewhere," she said. "A letter? A journal?" Did her father even keep a journal?

Archer stood at the door, his hands crossed over his chest. "Ivy, what do you think you will find after two years? A voice from the grave? You think an answer will save you, but it will only cut you anew. Don't go deeper into this forest. I fear what you might find."

She slammed a drawer shut and turned on him. "Is that what happened to you? You went deep into the forest and found only darkness?"

His eyes were hard, his mouth a thin line. Archer was harder to read now, under his beard. All through the night, she'd caught him staring at his own skin in fascination, though she hadn't been brave enough to ask him what he saw—or worse, if what he saw was himself, clearly, for the first time in months.

"Darkness isn't *only* anything," he said. "Once you let it inside, it's everything."

He was speaking in riddles again.

"Let it go, Ivy."

"No. There are only two options here. Either he was tricked, or he lied to the entire town. And I can't live with that."

"Then believe he was tricked." He shrugged, as if it didn't matter. But it did.

"It's not that simple!" Ivy cried. "Everything I've done—the life I've lived, accepting being cut off from the forest—it's because I believed my father when he told me it was dangerous. That no matter what I'd known growing up, that the forest had changed, and it was a threat to our lives. I believed him when he told me he tried to save you all, and you refused to leave."

"He did not," Archer said firmly. "At least, no one I know. Perhaps he told some, and they did refuse to leave."

"Like my mother?" Ivy lowered herself to the surface of her father's bed. Dust eddies swirled around her lap. "How is my mother? Don't think me a monster for saying it now. Even before the bells, I almost never saw her."

Ivy's mother hadn't even lived in Archer's village. When she left the town, it was to go into the wild, to range deeper and deeper into the forest to find the plants she loved more than her own family. Honestly, it wouldn't surprise Ivy at all if her mother had rebuffed her dad. There'd never been anything he could offer, promise, or threaten that would bring that woman out of the woods.

Archer was regarding her, his moss-green eyes soaked in sadness. "Ivy…" He joined her on the edge of the bed. "I don't think you're a monster. There is only room here for one of us."

93

"You aren't a monster."

"Oh, but I am. This magic… it's broken something inside. Forgive me, Ivy, please."

"What do you mean?"

"This whole night, I've been so callous. I played games with you when I should have been begging for help. I tricked you when I should have confessed every horrible curse. I bedded you, when by all rights you should have left me to die in the snow."

"Archer…"

"You're right. We should talk. For I haven't told you nearly enough of the things I've done—of the things the whole village has done to try to survive in the face of these bells." He sighed, and turned his face away, as if ashamed. "Before. The other solstice rites. Last night it was me. Last year, my brother tried. We thought—we thought maybe strength was the answer that time. That because he was a ranger, he could withstand the pain of battling the bells. But he could not."

Ivy leaned back as horror dawned inside of her. "And the year before that?"

"Your mother was the first to try. She believed that because she had connections on the other side— you and your father—that she could use her love to break the barrier and make it through to you." Archer breathed deep. "She was wrong."

eleven

TWO YEARS. Two years ago, on the solstice night, her mother had died in a vain attempt to bring down the barrier of the bells. Two years ago, on the solstice night, her father had walked into the barrier and perished as well. She'd never known why until now, but it made all the sense in the world.

It wasn't an act of despair or even an awful mistake. It wasn't a rare flower either, but something endlessly more precious.

"He was trying to save her." Ivy's voice was little more than a breath. "He must have seen her there, through the barrier. Maybe he even saw her dying. And he tried to help her."

"Your father?" Archer asked, incredulous.

She didn't need a journal. She already had the answers. "He loved her. He *always* loved her, even after she left us. I was just a child. I couldn't understand a mother who chose the forest over us. But my dad..."

She broke off. Her father had understood, the way Ivy never had, that the forest folk didn't belong to them. That they never, ever would. Her mother might spend a few years by her father's side, and Archer might claim to share her soul, but what difference did that make, in the end? Archer could have sex with her in the greenhouse or her bed or on a treetop deep in the forest, but that didn't make him hers. He could tell her he'd been faithful, all those years behind the barrier, but that didn't mean they could build a life together. He was forest, and she was town.

Archer's arms encircled her, and she breathed him in, and only wept harder.

Until yesterday, she'd never thought she'd see her mother again, but knowing it was true—that she was gone, that both her parents had gone together—somehow, it was different.

And maybe it answered some of her questions, too. Maybe Archer was right. After all, as he'd told her last night, his bell sickness hit hard and fast on that first day. As awful as it had been for her, it must have been instant torture for pure forest folk. Her father may have warned them about a barrier keeping them from the town, and they rejected him because why would they care about not being able to leave their precious forest? He said they'd laughed away his warnings about dark magic, and that made sense, too. Why would they mistrust their own home?

But since her father hadn't realized the true cost of the barrier bells, he wouldn't have warned them that the barrier would sicken them. When they discovered the awful truth, too late, of course, those who had been warned in advance might try to deny they ever had the chance to leave. She wouldn't be surprised if the leaders of the forest folk didn't say a word about her father's visit. So maybe Archer was ignorant of it, too.

And even if they'd once rejected the advice to leave, that didn't mean they couldn't change their mind. Her mother had sacrificed everything to try. And then Archer's brother, and then Archer himself. And though he'd survived, he'd put himself through hell to do so.

She craned her neck to look up at him, at the reddish stubble covering his neck and chin, at his sad, green eyes gazing down at her.

"You said my mother believed her love for us would help sustain her as she brought down the barrier. And I suppose she did love us, in her forest way."

Archer's brow furrowed and a frown tugged at his lips. "You believe the forest folk love differently?"

"I know my mother loved me differently than I loved her, differently than my father." A distant, fickle love that hadn't been enough to overcome the power of the bells, though Ivy supposed it meant something that her mother had believed it might.

"And what of me?" His arms had grown slack around her back and he drew back, regarding her warily.

"Yes," she prompted. "What of you, Archer? My mother offered her love; your brother, his strength. What did you possess that you hoped might overcome the bells?"

Archer pulled away from her then, turning his face to the floor. "I had nothing."

"I don't understand." She moved to put her hand on his shoulder, but he shied away.

"Everyone who had attempted the breach had died. But me? I had nothing to lose. The only people who still cared about me needed me to do this more than they needed me to do anything else. I could sacrifice everything I was in the service of dark magic, hone myself in evil enchantments. I could become nothing, until there was nothing for the barrier to burn."

"But you didn't." Ivy gave him a hopeful smile. "You dabbled in darkness, but you're still here, with me. Whatever strange magic possessed you last night, it's gone. We defeated it, you and I."

He looked back at her and lifted his hand to his sweater, as if cupping his heart, but when his fingers grazed the weave, he stopped. "I want to believe that dark magic can be defeated, but I've spent too long in the forest."

"In the depths, where magic reigns?"

He shook his head. "No. Within earshot of your evil bells. The worst magic is not native to the forest. It's born in the hearts of men."

There was a loud pounding at her door. "Ivy Potter! Open up!"

Deacon Ryder. Her least favorite councilman. Everything he said sounded so reasonable… until you thought about it. Back when her father was still alive, they'd go to services from time to time, but the last time she'd set foot in the chapel was at her father's funeral.

She shot out of Archer's arms. "Hide."

"He's coming into your father's bedroom?" Archer asked wryly, not moving.

True. Ivy wiped her eyes, and checked her reflection in the mirror. If she looked like she'd been crying, Deacon Ryder would certainly notice. Knowing him, he might even sniff out that she'd been participating in unwed fornication.

"Hide, Archer," she repeated. "This man hates forest folk."

"I hate him," he replied evenly. "I remember the things he said about me and mine when I came to visit. He thought us all devils." Archer cracked his knuckles. "Wonder what he would think of a little curse or two? I *am* devilish now."

"Don't you dare!" she whirled around and shoved him to the far corner of the room. "Just stay put. No sounds — and no curses, do you hear me?"

"I hear you," he murmured. "Your voice is drenched in fear. What do you think this man can do to me? I brought down the bells. I am not afraid of a preacher."

She didn't like his tone, nor the way his words made her hair stand on end. Even without second sight, Ivy suspected Archer's magic was rallying down his veins, and she had little doubt how dark it might be.

"Ivy Potter!" came the deacon's voice again.

"Coming," she called, as the deacon attempted to splinter her door. She shut the door of her bedroom tight, and hurried to the shop entrance.

Deacon Ryder stood on the stoop, his tall, thin frame bundled to within an inch of his life, and held by the collar a curious shepherd. "Ivy Potter, good morning. It seems Trapper here has taken an interest to something that came out of the woods and up your front porch."

"So it seems," she replied. "But like I told Mr. Beemer, I've got quite the lock on my door. Nothing is getting in here. I have to make sure I'm protected, you know, ever since my father died." She patted the dog's head and he pressed his nose into her palm, snuffling. Hopefully she could make him decide it was her scent, not Archer's, he was looking for. "Maybe whatever it was headed back into the forest."

The deacon eyed her and she could feel her puffy, tear-stained eyes tingle beneath his gaze. "Maybe. But that's the second thing I came about, Ivy. We must do something about the bells."

She feigned innocence. "*We*, sir? How might I help? Think dousing them with tea might start them up again?"

"Very funny, child," he said, his tone grave. "May I come in?"

"You may," she said blithely. "But Trapper and his muddy paws can stay in the yard." The last thing she needed was a dog sniffing out Archer in her father's bedroom.

The Deacon entered, and Ivy hung up his coat and scarf and offered him a cup of tea.

"None of your potions, Miss Potter," he said, looking down his nose at the jars of loose tea mixes lining her shop shelves.

"English Breakfast?" she trilled as she put the kettle on. Was that movement in the hallway to the apartment? *Careful, Archer.*

"You know, Ivy, we've been worried about you."

"Who has?"

"The community. All the way out here, away from all good company. Don't you think you'd be happier closer to the center of town and away from all these trees?"

"I'm happy not having to commute to my job," she replied, taking down a pair of mugs.

"And while the barrier's down—well, your mom is forest folk. Wouldn't want her coming out of the woods and snatching you."

The teacups clattered out of Ivy's hands. *Won't be a problem, Deacon. Turns out, my mother and father died the same night.* But what she said was, "I am not a child who can be spirited away and replaced with a creature of straw and mud, sir. You may have forgotten me out here, but time moves past just the same. I'm not even a teenager anymore." She poured the hot water over her tea bags and set the mugs on a tray with lemon, sugar, and cream.

The deacon took cream, and lots of it. The tea was nearly white by the time he brought it to his lips. Ivy grimaced and took a sip of her own plain tea. She'd almost forgotten what English breakfast tea tasted like—this was the first time in years she made herself anything other than redbell.

"Well," the deacon said after a moment. "What about your friend?"

She choked on her sip. "What friend?"

He clucked his tongue. "Ivy, I may be an old man, but I'm not a fool. Back before the barrier, you had a friend in the forest, did you not?"

She smiled as serenely as she could. "Many friends, sir. My father worked there, if you remember."

He sighed. "Yes. Many friends. I'll count it a blessing I was able to separate the youth of my town from such bad influences. What was your little boyfriend's name? Arbor? Arrow? Something wild and pagan."

Ivy's gaze traveled over her visitor's shoulder to where something wild and pagan stood in the shadows of the hall, watching her with moss-green eyes and a wicked smile.

"Archer," she replied. "I mean, I think that was it."

Archer frowned at her, and as the deacon leaned over to refill his cup, she rolled her eyes.

"Well, your father was quite concerned about him back then."

Ivy swallowed past the sudden lump in her throat. "My father knew Archer for a decade. What could there be to be concerned about?"

Deacon Ryder gave her a look. "What all fathers are concerned about for their daughters."

Somehow, she doubted it. Her dad was a scientist, not an overprotective reactionary. When she told him she and Archer were having sex, he'd made the appointment for her to get birth control himself. But she was not in the mood to argue about her father's beliefs with this man this morning. "It was only puppy love."

"Puppy love can be dangerous, too, Ivy. What if you'd ended up with a baby from your forest lover, as your father did?"

She set her cup down. "To be fair, Deacon Ryder, my mother had the baby, too."

"Yes, and see how that turned out." The old man gave a piteous sigh. "Many's the night when I counseled your father on how to manage, raising his daughter all alone while his wild wife did who knows what in the forest."

102

Ivy hadn't known that either, and she doubted the deacon's counsel included trips to the OB-GYN. "Thank you for being there for him, sir. I'm sure you helped him immensely, and I couldn't have asked for a kinder or more invested father." That, at least, was the truth. "He helped me understand my forest side, and my town side."

The deacon pursed his lips so hard Ivy wondered if the milk had gone sour. "Yes, I remember those days, Ivy. Your father was concerned he'd been too lenient with you. That you were growing wild like your mother. That your forest side would take you over. Blood will out, you know."

Her shoulders tightened, but she forced her tone into a lightness she didn't feel. "I'm here, aren't I?"

"Yes," he said simply. "As near to the forest as *humanly* possible. And now the barrier is down."

Ivy said nothing.

"You must promise, child, not to go into the forest. I won't have you trapped there when the bells begin to ring again."

A shudder passed over her skin. "You're repairing the barrier."

"Trying to," he replied. "It'll take a bit of work, unfortunately. The curse that brought it down was heavy indeed."

In the shadows, Archer beamed.

Ivy brushed imaginary dust from her pants. "Well, Deacon, I wouldn't want to keep you…" Wait. Maybe she *did* want to keep him. The longer the deacon remained, the longer she'd keep him from… doing whatever it was he needed to do to repair the bells.

And the deacon seemed in no rush to leave. "Ivy," he said in the voice of a man who'd delivered ten thousand sermons, "Do you know why we built the barrier of the bells?"

"Because the forest had grown dark and dangerous, and we had to protect the town from evil magic," she recited politely. Was it ever true?

"We always have to protect ourselves from magic, Ivy, evil or otherwise," he corrected. "And the rising perils the forest presented gave us an opportunity to do so."

An opportunity? Archer took a half step out of the shadows, and Ivy made a covert gesture at him to stay back. He frowned at her.

"I was never so blessed in my life as when it became clear to me that the time had come to reveal the evil of the forest for what it truly was."

"Excuse me, sir?"

"When this town was first founded, Ivy, it was nothing. Just a backwoods little speck. The settlers turned to forest magic out of desperation those early, lean years. They endangered their everlasting souls, yes, but they did it to survive. Can you imagine what might drive a people to that?"

Behind the deacon, Archer shrugged and nodded. Ivy had to agree. She understood, all right, but not nearly so well as her lover did.

"I thought the people of this town would never get over this original sin, this temptation of the forest and all the evil it contained. But times change, Ivy. You saw them change."

Yes, she had. The posters, the ridicule, the fear, the isolation she and her forest-blooded neighbors had faced as fear of their kind had grown in town and beyond.

"The forest was driving away business. Do you think Ernest Beemer could have built up his quarry—do you think big city investors would come into our town, open factories and chain stores and build apartment complexes and cell phone towers—if we were every second threatened by fairy tale monsters?"

"Well, no, now that you mention it…"

"Which is why we need to get this barrier back up. Cutting off the forest—it's made our town safe. Prosperous. Virtuous, too." He leaned forward and lowered his voice. "You don't know how many vigils I've sat for girls like you, Ivy. Girls that weren't so lucky to come away from their forest boys safe and sound. Girls with forest—" he made a face "—*things* growing inside them."

Ivy leaned away from him as a sour taste spread over her tongue. Had she, too, been a forest *thing* to the deacon when she was born? Was she a *thing* to him now, ever teetering on the edge of eternal damnation?

"It was vital that we protect kids like you from making these same mistakes. From making the same mistake your father did."

Ivy's brows knit as she stared at the older man. "Did you share these… concerns with my father?"

"Of course!" he cried. "Your father was my greatest triumph. A forest-lover to the core. You know that. His greenhouse? His forest girl? No matter what I told him about the evil he courted, I thought he'd never listen."

"But he did listen," she pressed, though something seemed to tug in the corners of her mind.

"Eventually. He saw the darkness rising in the forest, and he realized you were right."

"Yes. He did. And he saw you, growing closer and closer to that forest boy. And he knew he couldn't condemn you to his lonely fate. And while I fought for every soul in the town, I admit your father only fought for your heart."

There was a sound behind Deacon Ryder and he turned to look down the hallway, but there was nothing there, to Ivy's relief. She didn't need Archer to have heard that last part.

Ivy's mind was reeling. She'd thought her father had supported the creation of the barrier because of some dreadful thing he'd seen in the forest, but what if that were no more true than his story about warning the forest folk to leave before the bells began to ring? What if it was the deacon who'd convinced him to turn from the forest and the folk within... in order to protect Ivy?

"What are you saying, sir?" she asked softly. "Is there no wicked magic coming from the forest?"

"Of course there is!" the deacon hissed. "Every twig in that forest is the work of the devil!"

Careful, Deacon. I have a whole greenhouse full of twigs.

"I'd burn every last leaf to the ground if I could, but that's not necessary, as long as we have the bells. Blessings on those sweet, silver bells." He bowed his head in thanks. "So, you see how we need your help."

"Excuse me?"

"The bells have stopped!" the deacon cried, and bits of spittle flew from the corner of his thin lips. "The engine that drives their power has ceased. We need to jump start it."

"I'm a florist and a teamaker," Ivy protested. "Not a mechanic." Or a magician.

"You're a Potter," said the deacon. "That's what matters."

"What?" Ivy looked at him in confusion. "Whatever do you mean?"

But he didn't answer, because just then, Trapper the dog started barking his head off.

twelve

DEACON RYDER RAN FOR THE DOOR and Ivy cast one more look down the empty hall.

Damn Archer! Why didn't he stay put? She hurried after the deacon to find him tugging at the dog's straining leash. A second later, the beast sprang free, beelined around the corner of the shop and headed straight for the greenhouse.

The deacon pulled out his walkie-talkie and called for help, while Ivy shoved her arms into the sleeves of her coat and cursed dogs and overconfident forest men, in that order. If only her curses held weight, like Archer's could. She shook her head in frustration and followed after Trapper and the deacon, her boots stamping with a satisfying crunch through the icy powder. How lovely to hear the sound of ice crystals, after all these years of bells. Even the dog's howling sounded fresh and clean.

She turned the corner and stopped dead. Trapper had reached the greenhouse dome, and was up on his hind legs, his front paws splayed on the glass. He growled loudly, his long teeth bared, his ears flattened against his head. But there was nothing there.

At least nothing townies like them could detect.

"What do you see, boy?" The deacon asked. "What do you see?"

Ivy knew what *she* saw, right beneath the canine's front paws. There were smears on the glass — a handprint, the impression of a cheek. Her face flushed against the cold morning air and for a second she feared the Deacon could tell what those marks meant, that he somehow would be able to see that she'd had hot and dirty sex a few hours ago on the other side of the pane.

"There's something in your greenhouse!" The deacon whirled to glare at Ivy.

"It's locked," she insisted. And she had locked it, last night, after she and Archer had left. But that didn't mean Archer hadn't snagged a key and sneaked back inside while she and the deacon had been talking.

The crunch of boots behind her made them both turn, and Ivy's heart leapt into her throat at the idea of Archer revealing himself, but it was only Shawn Cooper from the tire shop, come to see what all the fuss was about.

"Look!" Shawn raised his arm to point at the dome. Ivy and the deacon both stared.

Something was rising from the surface of the dome like steam, if steam came in colors of violet and black, swirling up the legs of the dog like a fast-growing vine. The dog's howls turned to whimpers, and he tried to pull his paws off the dome, but couldn't. He jerked and flailed, arching his neck and looking back to his master with wide, fearful eyes.

"It's black magic!" the deacon shouted, backing up a few steps as the dog let out a high-pitched shriek. The smoke had covered the dog's legs and chest now, and was wrapping tight about his neck.

The others were rooted to the ground as if the snow were made of glue, but Ivy ran forward, shouting at the… thing that had the dog in its grip.

"Let go!" she cried. "Let go!"

But before she could reach it, it floated up into the air, taking the animal with it. The dog twitched as he floated, like a fish caught on a line, and the smokiness spread, choking out Trapper's hysterical whelps and making him jerk and writhe in terror.

"Dear God in heaven," the deacon whispered, as the smoke enveloped the dog's back and belly, and traveled down his hind legs. Any moment now, it would crest the roofline, and everyone in town would get an instant demonstration of what might happen now that the bells were silent.

Ivy crouched in the snow and jumped as hard as she could, grabbing the creature by his dangling tail, just as the smoke reached its tip. Her hair touched bristling fur and something cold as well water and dark as a grave.

Ivy…

The echo that roared through her bones was unmistakably Archer's.

And then she fell back into the snow, her bones jarring against the frozen ground, her arms full of German shepherd. He twisted out of her grip and turned to face her, half in a crouch, his head held low and ears folded flat.

"Trapper?" she whispered. But Trapper was not the beast that stood before her, growling and snapping impossibly long teeth. Its eyes were pure black, and its hair seemed to have grown several inches.

Ivy's breath froze in her lungs. Oh, no.

Archer? she thought at it.

It reared back as if to lunge.

"It's me!" she cried. "It's Ivy!"

"It's a demon!" screamed the deacon. "Kill it!"

Shawn fumbled in his waistband, and the dog-thing turned toward him and leaped. Shawn went down in the snow, a pistol tumbling out of his hands. Ivy scrambled to her feet but had no idea what to do. The beast was all claws and teeth and rage, a dark, furry blur on top of the screaming man.

A crack sheared through the icy morning, and the monster stilled and slumped on top of the man. Shawn pushed at it with bloody hands, and it fell to the side, a German shepherd once more.

There was a smoking gun in the deacon's hands, but Ivy had no time to think about it. She knelt in the snow next to them. Shawn was bloody and torn, with deep gashes on his forearms and large punctures on his face and throat. She moved to press her hand against the wound and he shied away.

"Don't touch me, witch," he hissed. "You set that thing on me."

She recoiled. "You need an ambulance." Her voice sounded calm. How odd.

Beside her, the dog wheezed and whimpered. His eyes had gone back to simple, doggy, brown. They were wide now, as if he had no idea how he'd gotten there, in the snow, with a bullet in his body and his

111

life draining into the snow. Gingerly, she touched his flank. At least there was one soul in town who wouldn't flinch away from her hands.

Deacon Ryder frowned in frustration. "Waste of a dog."

The bells were ringing again—no, wait, those weren't bells, but a siren. The paramedics arrived, shoving Ivy and Trapper aside to deal with Shawn.

The dog wheezed, but barely moved. As the others dealt with the man, Ivy carefully rolled Trapper over to see if the bullet had exited his other side.

A shadow fell across them both.

"Ivy?" Jeb's voice came from above. "What happened here?"

"I'll tell you what happened," the deacon butted in. "Some monster out of the forest possessed my dog and made it attack us. It was a mercy killing, I tell you."

"It wasn't a mercy killing," Ivy muttered. "Trapper's not dead."

The deacon took a few steps back, which was when Ivy remembered he was still holding a gun. This whole morning had gotten completely out of hand. Five minutes ago, she'd been sitting in her shop drinking tea and now she was tending to a dying dog, after pulling a demonic force right out of the air.

And Archer was still nowhere to be seen.

"Do you need me to run home and call the vet, Deacon?" Jeb was asking.

"I don't want anything to do with it," he replied. "Should be put out of its misery."

"Yes," Ivy broke in. "Call a vet. Can we maybe get Trapper in the back of your truck, Jeb? Let me grab some blankets and my purse—"

"Leave it be, Miss Potter," the deacon said. "You have no idea what might be contaminating its body right now."

"Mostly?" she hissed at him as Jeb hurried off to fetch his truck. "Bullets." She wouldn't treat a houseplant with as much disdain as the deacon was showing his dog. Whatever Trapper may have done to Shawn, it wasn't his fault.

It was… something else.

Deacon Ryder clucked his tongue at her. "You saw the same thing I did. Don't you care what this town is facing? A dead dog will be the least of our problems now that magic can leak out of the forest at will. What do we do when demons start possessing every person in town?"

Ivy shook her head and waited for Jeb to return. She wasn't about to leave Trapper alone with the deacon. He might try to finish the job.

"And I still want to get a look in your greenhouse, young lady. Whatever that thing was, it seemed to have special interest in whatever you've got growing inside there."

"My greenhouse is locked up tight, sir. And I'll kindly ask you to step off my property. I don't like men coming here and waving guns around." Especially not when they seemed more than ready to shoot anything that came out of the forest.

Deacon Ryder scowled, but moved off the property.

Jeb returned with his truck, and together, they lifted Trapper up into the bed. Ivy ran inside the shop to grab some blankets and her purse.

"Archer?" she poked her head into her bedroom, her father's room, the bathroom, her panic rising at every empty threshold. "Where are you?"

Just as she feared, there was no response. Back outside, the deacon watched them from the street as Ivy climbed in back with the bleeding dog. She pulled Trapper's head into her lap. He was still, his breaths coming in shallow pants.

"You'll be okay," she said, and searched his eyes, as if they might hold the secret. Archer's voice still rang in her mind, chilling yet undeniable.

As they rumbled up the road to town, she smoothed down the animal's fur, trying to make sense of everything that had happened that morning. Everything had happened too fast. The revelation about her parents' deaths, the intrusions from Mr. Beemer and Deacon Ryder, Archer's disappearance, and then…whatever it was that had overtaken the dog and attacked her and Shawn.

Whatever it was… because she couldn't bear to believe that vicious monster could have been Archer, no matter what she'd heard when she touched it.

~

At the vet's office, they whisked the dog away for surgery.

"You should go home, Ivy," Jeb said. "You look exhausted."

"Long night," she replied woodenly. But where had Archer gone? He couldn't have escaped to the forest already, not with all the men from the quarry patrolling the border where the barrier lay broken.

114

And he wouldn't leave without her, right? Without even *telling* her?

"What, couldn't sleep with all the silence?" Jeb asked her. "Can't say I had that problem. I haven't had such a restful night in years."

"Good for you." She played with the leather strap of her purse. She couldn't help but replay her conversation in the shop with the deacon, the way she'd dismissed and diminished her attachment to Archer. Puppy love, she'd called it.

He had to know she was lying to get rid of their unwanted guest. He had to.

Jeb was quiet for a moment, letting expectations pool between them. "What did the townies want out of you?"

Odd choice of words. "*We're* townies, Jeb."

"Why?" he asked. "Because we live on this side of the bells?"

She didn't want to answer that, so instead she said, "Beemer and Ryder came by to ask if I'd seen anything come out of the forest when the bells stopped. I told them I hadn't."

"That's what you told them, huh?" He nodded. "Good choice."

"It's the truth." She turned to him. "Why? Did you see anything come out of the forest?"

"Not me." Jeb raised his hands in defense. "Then again, my eyes aren't as good as they once were, Ivy girl."

She shook her head and donned her coat. Cryptic conversations with her neighbor wouldn't do her or Archer any good right now.

"Of course," he went on, his tone deceptively casual, "I never did have the sight as good as a full-blooded forest man, and those years drugging myself with redbell tea to stave off the effects of those bells probably killed any magic I had left. But—" he dropped his voice to a whisper, "—if I did have a touch of the sight left, I'd say you're glowing brighter than a midsummer fire."

She did a poor job of hiding her gasp and Jeb smiled in triumph.

"Nah, you didn't see anything come out of the forest. But I've no doubt you saw plenty, later on."

He might as well have waggled his bushy eyebrows at her.

She zipped her coat up to her chin and avoided his gaze. "You sound ridiculous," she said. "What do you take me for, some idiot townie girl who rolls over the second a fickle forest man snaps his fingers?"

The old man chuckled. "No, Ivy girl. You're the one who keeps saying 'townie.'"

thirteen

IVY WALKED HOME SLOWLY, marveling at the sound of her boots crunching through snow, of trees creaking beneath the weight of ice, and local birds chattering away in the boughs, the rare, crystalline silence of deep winter. It was all quite perfect, until she saw her house, and the yellow plastic tape stretched across her yard.

She ducked beneath the tape and stomped across the wintry lawn toward the greenhouse, heart in her throat as a series of horrible scenarios flashed through her mind. They'd found Archer. They'd killed him. Or maybe he'd called up his dark magic again and set it after the men of the town.

A dozen people milled around the door to the greenhouse, which lay splintered and hanging from the hinges.

"Hey!" she shouted, and they whirled around, ducking their heads in guilt as they caught sight of her. "What the hell did you do?"

"*Hell*, indeed." Deacon Ryder strode out of the group to block her path. "The council thought it prudent to do a thorough examination of the property after the demonic possession we witnessed here earlier."

"You broke into my greenhouse!" she spluttered, shocked into ineloquence by the violation. Would they have done the same to her father, or did they still think of her as a child, whose rights they could trample whenever they wanted? She drew herself up straight and when she spoke again, her voice was firm. If she could stand up to Archer's curses, she could stand up to men from the town council.

"What are your plans to repair my door? I have fragile plants in there that will be destroyed by the cold temperatures."

"I wouldn't describe the plants you have in there as fragile," said Ernest Beemer. "We've been at them for nearly an hour with axes, and we're hardly making headway."

"You're cutting down my crop?" she craned her neck to see over the crowd. "You have no right—"

The redbell. Her customers, the forest folk who needed her medicine…

"We're just trying to get in," Beemer said. "You've blocked the door."

"I have not—" She cut off as she caught sight of the wall of brambles filling the doorway, a knot of thorns as thick as her torso. Several branches had been sheared off but the entrance was completely closed.

"When was the last time you were even inside this place, Miss Potter?" Beemer asked from behind her.

118

"This wasn't here," she gasped. "I swear this wasn't here..." *Last night.*

"Don't you see, Ivy?" the deacon counseled, putting his hands on her shoulders. "There is magic coming from the forest again. We need to see what's inside the greenhouse and what danger it might pose to the town."

Archer. Archer must be inside the greenhouse. No wonder he didn't want these men searching. And Ivy didn't want it either, but they were all staring at her, as if she had the ability to make the brambles part.

"It's a *greenhouse*," Ivy said, giving her voice just a touch of derision. "Did no one think to break a window?"

"Gee, why didn't we think of that?" Shawn stood off to the side, bandages wrapped around his neck and arms. He looked eons away from the fellow who used to lob spitballs at her hair from the back of math class.

Don't touch me, witch. The whispered memory of *forest-lover* loomed large in her mind.

He pointed at one of the panes, which she now realized was broken, not that it made much of a difference, as brambles spiderwebbed thickly across the opening.

Ivy peered closer to see the tangle of thorns spread over every pane in the dome, completely blocking the view of the interior.

"There's something hiding in there," Shawn said now. "I know a nest when I see it."

"What have you got in that greenhouse, young lady?" Beemer demanded.

My forest lover, of course. There was nothing she could say to make them believe her. They knew who—and what—she was. "Plants?" she offered.

Someone came back with a chainsaw and no one even bothered to ask Ivy's permission as they buzzed through the brambles. The thorns had created a wall several feet thick, until it was as if they were drilling a tunnel, rather than a door.

Archer, be careful, she found herself begging, her hands squeezed into tight fists inside her coat pockets. When it was just two men, he'd set a dog on them. What would he do if a dozen penetrated the fortress he'd built?

The quality of the chainsaw's whine shifted as it finally broke through to the interior, and everyone stepped back, as if expecting something magical and horrible to burst forth. Nothing happened, even as the man working the machine carved out an opening big enough for a person to crawl through. It was dim inside, shadowy, as Ivy had never quite seen it. Like the inside of the forest itself.

All the men looked at each other. No one seemed ready to climb through. The air that floated out smelled of midsummer, green and brown and hot against their faces.

"Well?" Beemer crossed his arms and glared at Ivy. "What have you got in there?"

"My answer hasn't changed in fifteen minutes."

And still, no one moved, which just proved to Ivy that they had no plan at all. They'd expected an attack, and when none was forthcoming, they were at a loss.

"Gentlemen," she said, making her tone as authoritative as possible, "I believe you are mistaken. These are some overgrown brambles, nothing more."

"Thickets do not grow overnight, Ivy Potter, not even in your mother's enchanted greenhouse." Deacon Ryder peered into the depths. "This is forest magic."

"Maybe it's just the barrier," she suggested weakly. "The trees by the barrier died from the sound of the bells. Maybe it didn't kill the plants in here, protected as they were by the glass, but it... stunted their growth. And now that the barrier is gone, they are...making up for lost time? They are forest plants."

Shawn gave her an incredulous look. Okay, so it wasn't very well thought out.

"There is something making up for lost time," said the deacon, "and it's dark magic. Ready your weapons, boys."

"No!" Ivy held out her hands. "I won't have you all shooting up whatever is left of the crops in my greenhouse. I will go in." She straightened her coat and stood tall. She might be the only one safe to enter.

"Be careful, child," said the deacon. "You know not what might lie within."

He was right about that.

"Are you kidding me?" Shawn sneered. "She knows exactly what's in there. That forest-lover probably planted it herself. She's just been waiting for the barrier to go down so she could unleash whatever she's been cultivating in that greenhouse."

Ivy whirled on him. "Why would I need to wait for the barrier to go down, dimwit? The greenhouse is on *this* side."

121

"Settle down," the deacon placed a hand on her shoulder. "No one thinks you are doing dark magic, Miss Potter, regardless of your forest blood."

"Speak for yourself, Ryder," grumbled Shawn. "She sicced that dog on me this morning. I saw what I saw."

Ivy ignored him. This was the kind of guy who lived in this town. Was it any wonder she'd been celibate all this time? She put one booted foot inside the tunnel of thorns, but she didn't catch fire or turn to stone.

The hair on the back of her neck was standing at attention, but she refused to turn back. She had beaten Archer at his game of questions. She knew the rules of the forest. She was Puss in Boots and Jack the Giant-Killer, and she could do this. A few crouching steps, and she was through.

Okay, Archer. Where are you? Afternoon light filtered dimly down through cracks in the thicket, which had spread over the entire inside of the dome. She felt as if she stood inside a giant tumbleweed. She headed warily down the main path, keeping half an eye on the brambles above. Though they'd spread thickly over the surface of the dome and the entrance itself, the actual space of the greenhouse looked the same as always, like a terrarium of the forest frozen in twilight. She passed the spreading branches of the trees and turned the corner, well out of sight of anyone who might be watching from the door.

"Archer?" she whispered loud as she dared. And then, louder, "Everything looks in order. There's nothing out of place here except the brambles..." And then she caught sight of the redbell patch, far in the corner, and trailed off.

This was the origin. A great, gnarled bramble root spread from the center of the patch, straining against the curve of the dome and spreading up and outward. The root pulsed slightly, sending out curling shoots at intervals as regular as a heartbeat.

Ivy swallowed. "Archer…" Deep shadows lay at the heart of the plant's trunk, buzzing the barely-there black-violet of evil magic. Ivy shivered in the warmth of her greenhouse. Everything within her told her to stop, to run away, but even as she watched, she saw the roots hardening, thickening, and reaching farther into the patch of redbells and crowding out the flowers that her friends in town needed so desperately, that Archer had risked his life to gather for the forest folk.

So whatever this bramble-tree was, it couldn't be connected to him, unless he brought it out accidentally, a stray seed carried with him like a burr on an animal's coat. Perhaps it fell from him last night, and took root in the soil.

A seed…

She peered more closely, at the center of the tree, as memories of last night rose up before her, the way Archer had pulled away from her at the last moment, the way the dark magic that held him seemed to vanish in the night.

This bramble was not only Archer's fault, it *was* Archer -- the surplus of his evil enchantments she thought had drained away.

Her stomach turned; her blood chilled. The thorns enclosing the space creaked and groaned as they grew, choking out even the slivers of light that remained. The twisted branches of the bramble thicket took on sinister shapes in the shadows --

torsos and heads, half-formed limbs, and knots like eyes. The greenhouse—her parents' precious greenhouse—was no longer safe.

One step back, then another. Bramble-vines twisted across the floor, heading her way, five-fingered shoots reaching out like grasping hands.

Ivy tripped over a root and stumbled, and a dozen figures snapped to attention. For a second, everything was silent, and then a great roar as the bramble bent the bronze rods. Glass panes shattered, showering glittering shards all around her. She threw her hands over her head and sprinted for the door.

Flanking the opening they'd cut into the brambles were two humanoid shapes, bark and branches twisted into the shape of men, twigs curling like Archer's hair over thorny ears, facing each other and thrusting their woody hands into the space. Already, it was smaller than before, the brambles twisting to take control.

Roots seemed to rise on the path, and the leaves shuddered above her as she ran. New shoots erupted from the freshly-shorn edges, tightening the tunnel, and the creatures on either side seemed to glare at her with wood-knot eyes, as if daring her to try to make it through.

Distantly, on the other side of the hole, she saw the men backing away as twigs and thorns sprouted before their eyes.

"Help me!" she called to the men in the snow. "Keep it open!"

She squeezed her eyes shut and dove for the hole, not even caring when the thorns caught her clothes and hair and skin, crawling through the prickles and scrambling over the twisting vines.

Words seemed to whisper along the bark, just out of range of her hearing, or maybe in a language no human could understand.

She felt them reaching — no, it was the men from the town, they were pulling her out—hacking away with their axes and saws.

Ivy fell to the snow-dusted ground, and ice stung the scrapes on her skin. But she was out. She was free.

Pressing a hand to her chest, she rolled over to look back through the hole. The brambles closing in, shutting the greenhouse away in darkness once more.

"The redbells," she said softly, to no one in particular. Her entire crop was in there. With those... *things.*

"Do you see why we must be on our guard?" Ernest Beemer announced. "One day without the protection of the barrier and look what has come to pass. Animal attacks, the forest takeover of the entire Potter greenhouse... this must not be allowed to continue."

There was a murmur of agreement among all the men gathered there. Ivy pushed herself to her feet, unable to find her tongue or take her eyes off the place where the door to her greenhouse used to stand. The bramble vines bulged outward, cracking the frame and slithering like living snakes over the concrete threshold.

Everyone stepped backward, staring in a mix of horror and fascination as the vines advanced at their impossible rate, hardening into brown, woody branches before their very eyes.

Was it ever going to stop?

"Get back!" someone shouted. There was the sound of metal scraping concrete, and the men dragged up a piece of wrought iron fencing from the yard. They shoved it up against the opening, wedging the sharp edges into the crack where the threshold met the concrete of the path. The wood shrank back, scarring beneath the touch of iron, and stopped its spread.

"How long will this hold?" one of the men asked.

"You never know with magic," said Deacon Ryder. "We should set up a perimeter of guards to keep watch over—"

"Over my property?" Ivy cut in. "This is my land. I didn't invite you here, and whatever is growing inside there, it was contained until you took off the door and attacked it with a chainsaw. If there's a problem here, you caused it."

"Oh, so we should leave you alone to grow God knows what kind of forest plants?" Shawn asked. "People like you are a menace to the town, Ivy Potter. Your greenhouse should have been shut down years ago."

"I grow medicine inside," she snapped at him. "Medicine the people of this town need because of the side effects of the barrier."

"*I* don't need it," he scoffed. "And if that barrier is so difficult for you people, why don't you move away? Save us all a lot of trouble."

You people? She was so sick of hearing that. She'd heard it for three years, from neighbors and tourists and inside her own head. The bells weren't the problem, just the people affected by them.

126

They had it backwards, the tourists and the townies. Maybe *they* should all move away, and just let the forest—and the forest folk within— be. She was moments away from speaking the thought aloud when Deacon Ryder stepped between them.

"There, there," he said. "Every soul in this town has reason to wish for protection from the forest and its enchantments, and that holds especially true for those who are marked by birth."

"That's not what I meant—" Ivy began.

"This greenhouse is the least of our worries tonight," said Beemer. "Who knows what other breaches may have come from the destruction of the barrier. The Potter greenhouse is lost, that much is obvious. Let's use what resources we have to make sure other businesses in town aren't compromised. I want at least twenty men at the quarry."

Everyone started shouting about their own security needs, and eventually wandered off her property. Ivy made sure they were all gone and her gate was locked, then escaped into her house.

The shop looked exactly as she'd left it, so at least they hadn't gone into her home while she was away. She ran from room to room, checking in closets and under beds.

"Archer!" she called, no longer caring who heard. "Where are you?"

She couldn't believe he'd abandon her there, without even saying farewell. Unless last night was nothing more than a forest trick, and Ivy was nothing more than a fool to imagine anything else.

fourteen

WHAT HAD HAPPENED IN THAT GREENHOUSE? What had happened to the man she spent the night with?

Ivy was shaking, shivering with a cold that went beyond her wet and icy clothes. It seemed to come from her bones, from her blood. When she'd been with Archer last night, he was *her* Archer. No matter what she'd seen when he first woke, no matter what kind of dark magic he'd confessed to, she believed he could keep her safe.

But one look around that greenhouse and Ivy was no longer sure.

In the bathroom, she ran the taps as hot as possible until steam filled the space so she could hardly see her hands in front of her face. She stripped and stepped beneath the shower, wincing as the scalding spray hit her skin, scrubbing as if you could wash off magic like it was mud. When she finished, her skin was pink and her hair was plastered to her neck, but she felt no cleaner than before. Long bramble scrapes on her arms and neck and torso were proof enough of what she'd been through. Her fingers trembled as she touched them, and she shuddered as she toweled off and shuffled into her empty bedroom to dress, her mind whirling.

Ivy couldn't stop thinking about the stories she'd heard in the town square the summer the barrier was raised. The bramble men and the babies who weren't babies, the whispered rumors and the things that made even her father fear the forest…those things were real, they were growing in her greenhouse, and this time, they were Archer's doing.

And hers, too.

Yet Ivy couldn't regret any of the things she'd done. If the alternative was to abandon Archer to evil magic, she'd risk a hundred bramble trees. If it was to spend another night pouring tea and pretending her life hadn't ended at seventeen, she'd brave a thousand demon dogs. If everyone in this town was going to hate her anyway, she might as well be the forest-lover they all thought she was.

Another knock at the door. Ivy sighed and pulled a sweater dress over her head, scraping her damp hair back into a clip.

Deacon Ryder stood on the stoop, his face drawn tight. "Ivy. May I come in?"

What if she just said no? This was her house, her world, and they didn't even care.

But instead she opened the door wider, her focus on the floor.

"I have had your greenhouse examined thoroughly."

Ugh. Just stay away.

"The perimeter seems to be holding for now, so I've no fear that you are safe tonight."

"Tonight," she echoed, while thinking that she didn't need his fear. She'd been *safe* for three years, and miserable. Screw safe.

"But you can see that the events of today prove what a precarious position we are in. We must resurrect the barrier, as soon as humanly possible."

"Has anyone tried to contact the forest folk?" she asked abruptly.

"What?"

"This whole day," Ivy said, "when the barrier has been down. Has anyone tried to go into the forest to contact the folk living there?"

He blinked at her. "Why? Why would we do that? The forest is dangerous."

"Then the forest folk are in danger."

"It's the same danger they've been in for years." Ryder waved his hand, as if dismissing them. "Ivy, I know you think they are your family, but you don't know them. You certainly don't know what might have become of them now, locked away and subject every day to all the forest's corrupting forces." He came closer and petted her shoulder, as if it might give her comfort. "Trust me, child, if you were to meet someone from the forest, they would not have your best interests at heart. You cannot live so long in Hell without turning into a devil."

She squeezed her eyes shut. Archer had warned her using very similar words. Warned her that he'd become something other than himself, that he'd dabbled in dark magic enough to stain his very soul. And she'd thrown caution to the wind.

"This is a hard truth, but a vital one. It took your own father ages to reach this conclusion as well. But when he realized the truth of his ways, and the danger that his permissiveness toward the forest folk posed to you, his precious daughter... well, he knew it wasn't safe."

Ivy looked at him. "Are you saying that my father turned against the forest because of my relationship with Archer?"

"Your father did not want you in any danger," Ryder replied. "And you were in very great danger from that forest boy. Thankfully, George Potter was not so far gone that he couldn't help you, where he had failed to help himself."

Ivy stepped back, shaking her head in disbelief. "But Dad spoke in the town square about enchantments he'd seen, dark things coming out of the deep parts of the forest."

"Indeed." The deacon nodded. "What better advocate than someone who knew the breadth and depth of the dangers we faced? What more passionate warrior than a convert?"

Ivy's head began to hurt, and this time, there were no bells to blame. Her father had always known of forest dangers. She'd thought he'd started to fear a great, dark magic. But what if his fear was much more personal?

It wasn't the corruption of the forest Dad hated. It was Archer, and the way he'd corrupted Ivy.

All those months, she'd thought her father was so cool, so understanding. She'd told him things her friends would never dream of confessing to their parents.

And he'd told her to be careful, of course, to take precautions with her birth control and to remember that forest folk weren't the type to commit. But he'd never forbidden her from seeing Archer, even as the talk in town grew frantic. He knew it would have come across as hypocritical, after his own affair with Ivy's mother.

Archer had sworn this morning that George Potter had never warned the forest folk about the barrier. And maybe he hadn't, because to him the bells had been a way to keep Archer away from Ivy for good. His guilt in the months following, when the bells drove Ivy and the other forest-blooded townsfolk half-mad…

I'm so sorry, Ivy. I was only trying to protect you.

Her father had lied to her. Her father had lied to the whole town, then died on the first solstice after the bells began to ring.

How many others would need to die for this false protection?

She looked at the old man before her, the one who so feared the forest that he'd warped a father's love to help destroy it. "What do you want from me, Deacon Ryder?"

"There were three of us who made the bell barrier, my dear. Me, Beemer, and your father. Beemer brought the metal, I sanctified the bells, and your father crafted the design. Based on the greenhouse or something."

Ivy supposed that made sense. The lattice from which the bells hung did share that same tessellated shape as the Potter greenhouse. But the lattice of the bells remained intact, save for that one spot where Archer had broken through. It was the magic, and the sound, that had ceased. She must have still looked confused, as the deacon went on.

"But that was just construction. Construction was easy. It was the miracle which proved tricky."

"The miracle?"

The deacon coughed. "Yes. The seal we created between forest and town. The song of the bells. The hum of power. You've got forest blood—you know what I mean."

Did she ever. Time was, she thought her skull would split open, it was so *miraculous*. "The magic," she said. "You mean the magic."

"Not magic!" he snapped at her. "Miracles."

Yesterday, she'd stood in this shop and told some skeptical tourist that it depended on who told the story whether her tea was medicine or magic. Apparently the same conditions applied when it came to miracles.

Archer had been right. The bells were a curse, same as the kind he'd used to break it. He said there'd been sacrifices—pain, anger, power. Dark magic needed to overcome the dark magic those three men must have wrought.

"We needed three to make the miracle work," the deacon went on. "Me, Beemer, and your father, again. Three of us to perform the miracle."

Magic, Ivy silently corrected. *Dark magic*.

"I wanted to protect the soul of this town. Beemer wanted to protect its future. And your father…" Ryder gave her a weak smile. "He wanted to protect you."

And instead he ruined her. Ruined everything that was good about their lives, and their friends, and his very livelihood.

"He loved you so much."

Perhaps. But it was a wretched kind of love that would destroy something to protect itself. A weak love, like a forest plant transferred into a plastic pot. Ivy crossed her arms over her chest and squeezed, but the shiver had started up again, bone-deep and chilling.

"And now I need your help, Ivy. We can't let your father's work be in vain."

It was already in vain. For separating her from Archer hadn't worked. She loved him still, no matter what he might have become, locked away in the forest.

"Beemer and I—we believe we can perform the miracle again, but only if it's still the three of us."

Ivy looked at him, confused. "My father's dead."

"Beemer thinks you'll do. You have your father's blood."

"You want my *blood?*" she asked, gaping. "You are standing in my shop and asking me for my *blood?*" She shook her head, slowly. "How can you lie to yourself like that, Deacon Ryder? You must know what it is you are really doing."

His expression turned hard. "Listen, Ivy…"

"No." She straightened. "I do not do dark magic. I want to protect the town as much as you, but I have seen what dark magic does to a person's soul. My father was haunted by the harm he caused. I saw it every day on his face after the bells began to ring, and now I know why."

She saw it on Archer, too, but the deacon didn't need to know that.

The deacon opened his mouth as if to speak again, but she was saved from hearing his lecture by another knock on the door.

Jeb stood on the threshold, the dying light of the afternoon casting his face in shadow. "Ivy, I saw the deacon's car out front. I've got his dog…"

"It's still alive?" the deacon whined from behind her.

Jeb gave Ivy a look, as if to say there was a reason he'd brought the creature to her house instead of Ryder's.

"Yes," she fairly hissed at him. "*He* is still alive, thanks to surgery."

Ryder shook his head. "I don't want it. I won't have it in my house."

Ivy bit her lip. This man had shot his dog this morning, and he deigned to talk to her of love and protection. "Then you'd better leave my house, Deacon, as I'm about to have Jeb bring Trapper in here."

Deacon Ryder looked like he wanted to say more, but Ivy took off, pulling old blankets and towels out of the closet. He stood there for several minutes, so Ivy took her own sweet time making up Trapper's bed. The most pitiful of all the creatures in their town would find a place to stay with her tonight. She didn't care what Deacon Ryder thought—what anyone in town did. To her she was a forest thing, contaminated like this dog. She could obey their evil laws and recite their evil rules and listen to their evil bells, but it wouldn't change the way they saw her. And perhaps they were right, too. For she'd spent three years pretending she was one of them, and it clearly wasn't true.

"I'll be back in the morning, Ivy," he said at last. "Think it over."

She did not respond, nor did she breathe easy until she heard his car start up on the street. How odd, that she could hear things like car engines now. It had been years since she could hear anything but the bells.

But tonight, she heard everything clearly—the thoughts in her head, the beating of her heart. The Ivy she'd been trying so hard to be peeled away like onion skin, and she heard, for the first time, the Ivy she had been meant to be.

Jeb carried the beast inside and lay it down on Ivy's makeshift dog bed near the stove. "I'd take him home with me, but you know my old cat, Midnight, won't suffer the presence of canines," Jeb explained.

"Poor Midnight," Ivy replied. "We certainly can't invade her home so close to Christmas."

"What did the deacon want with you?" Jeb asked. "And what's with all that yellow tape around the greenhouse?"

Questions without answers. "It's been a long day, Jeb. A long, strange day."

Jeb studied her, and she recalled what he'd said at the vet's. It had been joking then, but Ivy didn't feel so lighthearted now. She knew what lived inside her greenhouse. She knew who was responsible for the horror of the bells.

And she couldn't tell this old man any of it.

Instead, she heated up some soup and some tea—not redbell, thank heaven—and sat with Jeb while he went over the vet's discharge papers. Trapper was still out cold from the sedatives, and probably wouldn't want to get up all night.

136

And he certainly wouldn't be able to protect her if whatever was in the greenhouse decided to come out. Ivy shivered and wrapped her hands around her mug. She seriously thought about asking Jeb to stay the night.

But what good would it do? A retired woodsman was no match for enchanted bramble vines and forest evil. And Ivy would never forgive herself if her actions hurt anyone else in town.

After dinner, when the darkness had settled over forest and town, Jeb left. She locked up behind him, pulling her drapes against the night and the silence beyond. All that quiet beyond. It made her head roar. At last, Ivy put on some soft music and puttered about the shop, keeping her hands and feet busy in hopes that it might quiet her mind.

It didn't.

In the absence of the bells, her thoughts roared—her father and the bells, Archer and his enchantments, the townspeople and their fear, and the choices that lay ahead of her. The rest of the town would stop at nothing to fix the barrier—that much was certain. All they'd have to do would be to point at the danger in her own greenhouse.

And what was she going to do about her greenhouse? If the barrier was fixed, she'd need her redbell, which means they'd need to do something to destroy…whatever it was growing from the bed. Though she'd promised the redbell to Archer to take back into the forest.

Archer, who had vanished into thin air.

Ivy put her hands on the sink, letting her head drop as the breath whooshed out of her. The cuts on her arms and face stung, her head ached, and her heart felt sore inside her chest. Twenty-four hours ago, she'd promised herself she would leave this town and this forest behind. Maybe she should keep that promise, now more than ever.

Behind her, Trapper let out a little whimper. Even without a bullet wound, she knew exactly how the poor dog felt.

Ivy... Something breathed ice at her back. *At last...* She spun around.

The man who stood in front of the stove was Archer, but not Archer. He wore no clothes, and his eyes were swallowed up in black. His muscles were drawn tight beneath his skin, and his reddish hair stood wild on his head, like he'd been struck by lightning.

"That," said a voice that cut the air to ribbons and sounded just enough like Archer to freeze the blood in her veins, "Took longer than I would have liked."

fifteen

THE COUNTER WAS COOL AND SOLID against Ivy's back. She gripped it with all her strength, as everything else tumbled away. The very floor of her shop seemed to tip toward the apparition before her, the terrifying not-Archer thing who stared at her like a ravenous beast.

She swallowed. "Archer."

"Did you miss me, my love?" There was a coldness there. Something alien, inhuman.

"So we are playing questions again." She kept her tone neutral.

This brought him up short. "I am not here to talk, Ivy Potter." And then suddenly, he was only inches away, and his hands were twined in her hair, and his lips hovered over hers. She froze, terrified, trapped under his awful, endless, black gaze.

I am Puss in Boots. I am Jack the Giant-Killer.

It did no good. "What do you want, then?"

"I want to kiss you," he said, quite reasonably, and then, "I want to eat you alive."

She wrenched her head away. "Stop! Let go of me!"

His hands fell to his sides and he stared at them, unblinking, his brow furrowed as if they did not quite belong to him. "We are alone at last," he said flatly. "It took all day."

She backed up a single, precious step, replaying the many hours since he'd disappeared. "Wait — are you saying you were stuck inside Trapper… all day?"

He looked at the dog, the poor, wretched thing. "You didn't seem to want to let him die. I had no choice."

"You possessed him," she said, as if saying the words made it any less bizarre. "You made him attack."

He chuckled then, and raised his hands in surrender. "It is hard to remember what one should or should not do in the thrall of dark magic. Won't you kiss me, Ivy Potter? I seem to want you to very badly."

She shook her head, to convince herself. She couldn't kiss this black-eyed thing. "What happened to your clothes?"

"Why do you care?" The corner of his mouth turned up, but the smirk didn't look the same on his face. "You like my body bare."

She flushed all over. "I…"

"Can't deny it," he finished, triumphant. "Come and kiss me. It was good for you last night."

Last night. Last night he had kissed her before he'd said a word, almost out of instinct, and his eyes had turned normal again. The more he'd touched her, the freer he'd grown from the darkness wrapped around his soul. And when they'd made love in the greenhouse, he'd been released entirely.

Of course, her greenhouse had been the one to pay the price. What would have happened if he had come inside her?

But he wasn't nearly so dark then as this wild thing that stood before her. Every time Archer let himself be overwhelmed by his own dark magic, it seemed to consume him more. If she let him touch her, it might choose her instead.

But even if it did, she couldn't leave him here, suffering, crying out for her in this odd, twisted way.

"What do you mean, you had no choice about Trapper?" she asked him.

Archer turned to look at the sleeping animal. "We were shot. I could have left, but without my magic, he would die. You were there—so sad, so sad." He turned back and cocked his head at her. "You didn't want him to die. I huddled in close and kept him alive. The time passed very quickly, I must admit."

"That would be the anesthesia." She crossed her arms over her chest and tried to find a place to look at Archer that didn't either freak her out or turn her on. Below the waist was totally off limits, and bare chests and hands were causing problems, too. But his face—it scared her, not least because it didn't scare her as much as it should have. "You are telling me you possessed the dog to keep it from dying."

"No," he replied. "I possessed the dog because it was causing problems. I remained inside to keep it alive."

"I think possessing an animal is generally a bad idea, Archer."

"You only say that because you've never tried it." He grinned at her. "You have never torn out the throat of a hare with the bite of a wolf. You've never soared through the night on an eagle's wings, or unhinged your snake jaw to swallow a rat whole."

Bile rose in her throat. Had Archer done all those things, in training to tackle the bells? Was this what her town had driven him to? "That sounds terrible."

"Even the eagle?" He raised his eyebrows over coal-black eyes. "How can you lie like that? Every man ever born wished that he could fly."

"I'll take a plane," Ivy said. "It costs less than the price you pay."

"But then you're trapped inside a metal tube."

She lifted her chin. "And what are you trapped inside of?"

Archer fell silent for a moment, and looked down.

Ivy already knew the answer. He was trapped in himself, a web of dark magic that twisted every thought, every word, that made him insult and frighten her even as he knew she was his only salvation.

"Come and kiss me, Ivy Potter," he repeated, staring at his hands. "Please."

It was the "please" that did her in, that broke her resistance like a twig snapped in the wind. She came a step closer, then another. He reached for her, and she stilled.

"Hands at your sides, please."

His arms dropped, balled into fists near his hips. But she wasn't looking at his hands, or his hips, or the

142

cock that jutted between them, semi-erect and pointing right at her.

She swallowed as she reached him, and grazed his jaw with the side of her hand. He winced as if burned, but did not move.

Somewhere inside lay her Archer, her sweet and laughing boy. Somewhere behind this darkness, underneath this cruel creature. It was him who called to her, who begged her to touch him, to kiss him.

"Shall I close my eyes?" he teased. "Or will you have me like this?"

"Hush," she whispered, and stroked his face again. The rosy hairs on his cheek were soft and downy, not scratchy like most men's stubble. She brushed her knuckles against it like petting a cat, and his eyes fluttered closed, a sigh bubbling up from his chest.

"You are stalling," he said softly. "Do I disgust you so much?"

"Not at all," she replied. "But you already know that, don't you?"

Their lips fit together the way petals enfold a rose, and as she sealed her mouth over his, his breath caught in a gasp. She slid her tongue inside his bottom lip, gently, slowly, and lingered, her head tilted up to his, hanging on as if the kiss kept her upright. And maybe it did.

She squeezed her eyes shut as his memories assaulted her senses. *The burning pain of bullets, the dog's amorphous terror, the urge to flee, and then... Ivy's hand on his head, his neck, her words soothing shapeless into the animal's mind.*

His arms twitched as if to grab her, but stayed locked at his sides.

143

She pulled away and blinked up at him, as if coming out of a dream. "Archer…"

His eyes were closed, his face still.

"Look at me."

"No." The word slipped out on a puff of air.

Ivy's hands ran along his shoulders, squeezed his arms. "Look at me, Archer."

He took a shuddering breath, and then another, as the muscles in his arms bunched and flexed, as every sinew of his body drew taut as a bow. He was hard as a rock, now. She could feel his length against her thigh, and a throbbing began between her legs in response, a gush of wetness she'd bet anything that Archer, with his forest senses, already knew about.

As if to prove it, his nostrils flared, and his lips parted, but his eyes stayed stubbornly closed.

She lifted on tiptoes and pressed her mouth to his again, and this time the tip of his tongue slipped out to meet hers, and she moaned in surprise and pleasure.

"Yes," he hissed against her lips. "Do that again."

"I'll do whatever you want," she promised, the words rumbling between them. Her legs felt weak, as if they would not be able to bear her weight, but she knew she was strong, stronger than the curses he used, stronger than the darkness shrouding his soul. Ivy wrapped her arms around his neck and drew him closer. "Just come back to me, Archer."

His tongue delved deep into her mouth at that, drawing out another rewarding moan, and he pressed his advantage, angling his mouth against hers and taking everything she offered. Lost in the kiss, she barely registered when his hands grazed her sides, and only moaned more as they ran up her body to cup her breasts. His thumbs flicked at her nipples through the weave of her dress, then pinched hard to bring them to bud.

"Gentle, Archer…" she begged, and he turned her in his arms and pushed her up against the wall of shelves. Glass jars rattled at her back and the cabinet knobs dug into her spine. His cock nestled between her thighs, his hips pumping ever so slightly, just a steady, subtle friction.

"Open for me," he demanded, his voice low like distant thunder.

She kept her legs closed and held his face in her hands, tangling her fingers in his wild curls. His tongue battled with hers now, taking her mouth in a crude imitation of what he so clearly wanted to do. His hands slid down and gripped her ass, then yanked up the hem of her dress and found their way inside.

At the touch of his fingers between her legs, she pulled away, reality crashing down.

Archer dropped his head to her shoulder, panting hard. "You're so wet."

Her legs trembled beneath her and she gripped his shoulders, but it was no use. Her thighs were parting as if of their own accord and he pushed his fingers in deep. She gasped.

"You want me," he said, thrusting his fingers in and out. "Feel how much you want me."

"I do," she admitted, as his thumbs brushed the sensitive nub between her legs. "I do want you, Archer. Ah—!" Ivy jerked as he rubbed too hard. "Wait. Stop. Archer…"

"Why should I stop?" he asked pleasantly, nudging his knee between her legs, "When every cell in your body begs for my touch?"

Ivy forced herself to breathe, to take a heartbeat or two and remember what this was all about. "Look at me. Please."

He raised his head and stared at her, a smug, little smile twisting his lips. His eyes were black as pitch.

Ivy shoved him away and pulled down her dress.

"Do you think you can cure me with a kiss?" Archer asked now, his tone cold and triumphant. "Foolish girl. I've cut curses so deep, they're etched on my bones. Every touch of magic burns more of my soul. If you really want me, you're going to have to do better than that."

She stared at him, breathing hard, her body vibrating like a plucked string. Her thighs were wet with want, her mouth bruised, her mind screaming his name.

"Come along, Ivy Potter," he sneered at her. "I thought you'd do whatever I wanted. And they say we forest folk are the fickle ones! What's a bit of black magic to scare you away?"

"I'm not scared," she said, and hoped it wasn't a lie. She could hear the desolation lurking just below his words. Her Archer was in there, and the only thing that scared her is that she might not be able to get him out.

The deacon claimed what he and Ernest Beemer and her father had done to the town and the forest was done out of love. Love for her, love for money, love for tradition — but Ivy knew it couldn't be true. The barrier was black magic, and if fairy stories taught you anything, it was that black magic held no power in the face of true love. Lust it might abide, but she and Archer were more than that.

"You're terrified," he shot back, mocking her. "You saw the gift I left in the greenhouse. You know what I'm capable of."

"The bramble-men tree," she replied, in a voice as calm as she could muster. "Yes. It was… enlightening. As a student of forest botany, I'm glad to know their origin at last."

He laughed mirthlessly. "That lesson nearly cost you your life."

Ah, so he'd seen something of her day when he'd kissed her as well. That made things simple. She wouldn't have to spend any time telling him about it. "I worry less of that than the effect it's had on the townsfolk. They are determined to resurrect the barrier."

That hit home. She saw him quake, saw the cracks at his seams. He'd risked so much to stop the bells, but it hadn't made a difference. A second later, the darkness rallied. He stood straighter than before, and smirked at her.

"Maybe they're right to fear the forest's magic, after all. Give us half a chance, we'll tear you to pieces."

Ivy's heart skipped a beat, but she forced herself to remain calm and spread her hands. "And yet here I stand."

"Yes." He snorted. "And what will you do?"

She took a deep breath. *I am Puss in Boots. I am Jack the Giant-Killer.* "I told you. Anything you want."

He blinked—a flash of green—and seemed to stumble, though he hadn't taken a step. A frown crossed his features.

"I love you, Archer."

He flinched, and the shadows buzzed violet-black around him. "You can't even see me. Blind, idiot townie girl. You have no idea what you're dealing with."

"You're right." She nodded. "But you're Archer. So I don't care."

Now it was his turn to step back, to retreat until he hit the tea counter. She seized the opportunity, coming right up to him and cupping her palm around his face.

He pushed his cheek against her hand, his black eyes widening in wonder. "You love me," he whispered in disbelief. But it wasn't a question. They weren't playing games.

"Yes."

His hand closed around her wrist, tight, frantic. "Then save me."

sixteen

ARCHER KISSED HER AGAIN, deep and desperate, as if she were a remedy and he were drinking her down. By the time he pulled away, Ivy could hardly breathe. Her skin felt on fire, and she shook with a need so base, she didn't care what color eyes he had or what kind of enchantments shivered along his skin and flowed through his veins.

"Take your dress off." He stepped back, leaning against the counter and folding his arms. His chin tipped up in challenge.

She crossed one arm over the other as she took the hem in her hands and pulled it off in one long movement, tossing it to the floor and standing before him, naked.

His gaze seemed to travel the length of her body, but it was tough to tell in that sea of black. Her nipples hardened beneath his perusal, and the air cooled the wetness at the juncture of her thighs.

"I am glad to see you've lost your taste for underthings."

"I didn't have a chance to put them on this evening." Ivy resisted the urge to place her hand over her crotch. "Now what?" She was in real trouble if he wanted her to dance for him or something ridiculous like that.

The firelight flickered at his back, casting his face in shadow, though she was sure he could see every inch of her flesh in stark relief.

He straightened, casually, and strode forward, circling her like a buyer examining a piece of merchandise. He was aroused, but calm. She didn't think he would even touch her. This was what a forest girl looked like at midsummer fires, naked before flickering flames. In the silence of the bell-free night, Ivy could almost pretend she heard the sound of forest drums. When they'd been teenagers, Archer had taken her away from all that, to their own, private, special space. Would this Archer be so considerate? Would he even think about what she needed?

He came around to her front, clamped his hands round her waist, and hoisted her up onto the counter. Then he stepped back, regarding her as one might a work of art.

"You are quite beautiful, Ivy Potter."

"Thank you." Ivy could say the same about him. Firelight was the only thing he should ever wear. It ignited the red streaks in his hair and beard, and made his pale skin glow like the sunrise. Even wrapped in enchantments, he was magnificent, a creature carved of myth. But he was too far away. She sat with her legs dangling over the side of the counter. The stone was cool against her butt, and it was hard to resist the urge to hop down and wrap herself around him.

"Touch your breasts," he ordered.

She blinked in surprise, then leaned forward. "Why don't you?"

Archer was silent, and those black eyes were a mystery. What was he thinking?

She sighed and cupped her breasts in her hands, lifting them and rolling the nipples beneath her thumbs. Her mouth parted and her eyes half-closed in pleasure.

"Are you imagining it's me?" he asked wryly.

"Of course," she murmured. Her inner muscles clenched as she continued to caress her breasts, picturing him watching her.

"You do that a lot, I assume."

Her eyes snapped open to meet his. "What do you mean?"

He shrugged. "Last night you said you hadn't been with anyone in three years. You must be quite adept at pleasuring yourself, then."

She nodded. "I suppose I am."

Archer's throat moved, as if he was swallowing, and his voice sounded rough when he spoke again. "Show me."

He couldn't actually mean...

"Lay back on the counter," he went on, pointing, "spread your legs, and show me."

Well, Ivy had said she'd do whatever he wanted. She leaned back on her elbows, drawing her knees up and bracing her feet on the counter.

"Spread your legs, Ivy," he coaxed from his spot halfway across the room. "Let me see all of you."

She squeezed her eyes shut and did as she was told. Her hand drifted between her legs, her fingers parting the damp folds.

"That's right." Was it her imagination, or did he sound a bit breathless? "Touch yourself."

She inserted a finger and drew it out again, slick with moisture, and circled it around her clit.

"Touch yourself the way you have these past few years without me," he urged.

"Why?" she asked him, without stopping the motion of her hand. "Why would I do this when you're right here?"

"Because I said so."

Ivy opened her eyes and tilted her face in his direction. He stood there, his hands tight at his sides, the tension evident in every muscle and sinew. Veins bulged at his neck and he held his jaw so tight it might crack. Odd, she would have thought he'd be stroking himself, too.

"Don't watch me," he ordered.

"Why not?" she asked innocently, as she trailed her finger up and down her folds, teasing her opening. "I'm picturing you."

He sniffed dismissively. "You aren't picturing this."

"Yes, I am. I want you, Archer."

It was like he was peering at her through a dirty screen, puzzling something he couldn't quite make out. "You pushed me away."

She bit her lip. He'd surprised her, was all. He'd kissed her so tenderly, she thought for sure she'd broken through. "I—"

"Don't speak if what you'll say is a lie."

Her mouth snapped shut.

His mouth split in a cruel grin. "You don't want me. You want the boy you knew."

"Archer—" She began to sit up.

"Keep touching yourself. Don't you dare stop."

She lay back down and spread her thighs more, giving him as good a show as she could manage.

"I'm not that boy anymore," he went on. "That boy who brings you flowers and treetops."

That wasn't true. He would always be that boy. *Her* boy, her Archer.

"Now, I'd throw you down before the fire and take you hard, Ivy Potter. You know I would."

She whimpered, and he seemed to find the sound satisfying.

"Good." He came closer, looking down at her, his black gaze sending shivers of dread and delight down her limbs. "Use two fingers."

She obeyed.

"Deeper."

She gasped. "Archer, please…"

He shut his eyes, as if he was at war with herself, and lay his fingertips on the counter, almost, but not quite, touching her. "I wonder what would happen," he said suddenly, "if I opened the shades?"

Her eyes widened. He wouldn't dare. She was lying on the counter, in full view of the street.

"I bet every man in town is guarding watch over the forest tonight, marching back and forth in front of your house. Don't stop, Ivy."

She growled, but kept going. An unbearable pressure built up inside her, a spring coiled tight.

"I could cloak myself in shadows. No one would see me. But oh, they'd see you." His voice seemed to break on the words. "Spread out on this counter like the most delicious feast. Your hair tossed wildly, your mouth swollen and wet, the sound of your moans."

Ivy moaned just then, as if on cue.

"Tell me truthfully, townie girl," he drawled, "You didn't wait for me all those years."

"I did," she gasped. "I swear. I love only—"

"Don't lie to me." His voice was sharp as a knife. "I saw the men in this town looking at you today. What would they do, do you think, if they saw you here like this?"

She stopped then, and covered his hand with hers. "Don't, Archer."

He shoved away from the counter, hissing as if she'd burned him.

She sat up, swung her legs back over the side, and regarded him. It wasn't the men in town Archer was trying to tease with the sight of her, awash with pleasure and just out of reach. It was himself.

"I didn't tell you to stop." His head was turned away, his voice directed to the floor. He wouldn't touch himself, he wouldn't let her touch him. He wanted her to save him but the monster inside wouldn't allow it.

"I didn't sleep with anyone," she replied. "You know that. I didn't even want to." She stepped down from the counter.

"Stay back."

"I won't lie to you. You cannot make me."

His hands tightened into fists. "I said, stay away from me."

But Ivy hadn't moved. "I want you, Archer, whatever you are. Because we have the same soul. I'm in there with you, and I won't be whole again until you're free."

He leaned against the other counter, his shoulders caving inward. "Please..." he begged, but couldn't put the request into words.

"I love you, Archer. You can't make me feel shame about it." She took one tiny step forward, and when he didn't move, she tried another. "Everyone in town tried when we were young. They called me a forest-lover, they told me I was foolish."

Archer sounded like he was having trouble breathing, like he was locked in an invisible battle.

"And all these years with the barrier, when I thought I'd never see you again, when I feared you'd been consumed by dark magic—"

"I had!" The words burst out of him like a curse, but he still shied away from her.

"All those years, if I'd been told how to save you, I'd have stopped at nothing." She laid a hand on his chest and pushed him back against the counter. "And so I will stop at nothing, Archer, to save you tonight."

He raised his head and looked at her, with eyes of gorgeous moss-green. His face was full of hope, and fear, and unspoken pleas.

Ivy's palms spread out over his chest. She could feel his heart beat beneath his skin, wild and quick like an animal.

"Trust me," she breathed, running her hands down his torso, over old scars and rippling muscles. She dropped to her knees.

Some great, guttural cry of need escaped from Archer as she wrapped her hands around his cock. He reached for her head, then whipped his hands away. "Please," he rasped, frenzied, "You don't know."

"Trust me," she murmured against the head of his cock. Gently, she pulled his foreskin back, and kissed the tip, laving her tongue around the rim. Archer groaned, and she felt his hands brush her hair, then vanish again.

"It's okay," she murmured, trailing kisses up and down his length. "Grab me if you like."

"Don't say that," he begged, his words barely human, "unless you mean it."

"Archer-mine," she cooed against his twitching flesh. "I mean it." Then she opened her mouth and took him in.

His fingers wove into her hair, fingertips against her temple, her cheek, her throat, so he could feel the muscles shift as she moved along his length. He tasted salty and dark, like the deepness of the forest, and she felt him growing even harder and longer in her mouth, as she gripped the base of his cock in her hands and pumped it in time to the movement of her mouth, sliding his foreskin forward and back with her lips.

His hands tightened and released on her head in subtle echoes of her own movements, guiding her to the depth and rhythm he liked best. "That's it, Ivy. Suck me…" and then language seemed to abandon him, and all she heard were gasps and growls.

You are mine, Archer. She weighed his balls in her hands, and squeezed the base of his cock as she took him deep. *I will never let you go.*

They couldn't cast the spell on the barrier without her help, and she would never give it. Ivy belonged to Archer and he to her, and neither the town nor the forest nor the darkest magic in the world was ever going to part them again.

She sucked and licked him, feeling his hips flex into her face, his stomach muscles tremble and his balls grow tight.

"Ivy!" he cried, and grabbed her by the shoulders, dragging her up his chest. She kept hold of his cock, slick now with her saliva, and he thrust into her hands, burying his face into the crook of her neck, covering her hands with his own. "Yes, please, oh, Ivy, Ivy, Ivy-mine…"

He shifted his hips to the side and she felt him jerk against her, coming at last with a long and keening cry. Something dripped, warm and stinging, over her hand and she pulled away even as he tightened his arms around her in a giant bear hug.

"Ivy." It wasn't a word. It was barely a sound, but she felt it in her bones. "Ivy."

"I'm here," she replied, stroking his hair with her clean hand. "I'm yours."

He lifted his head and smiled at her, a real smile, an Archer smile, full of charm and laughter and light. And then he kissed her, full-lipped and free. She searched his eyes and saw nothing but green, and she pressed her cheek to his chest to listen to his heart beating, steady and true.

He dropped his lips to her hair, murmuring words she couldn't quite make out. Her eyes drifted closed and she breathed him in.

Firelight, bright and cozy. A warm and willing woman in my arms.

This time, I must make it last.

seventeen

IVY MUST HAVE STIFFENED SLIGHTLY, as Archer's arms grew firm around her and he captured her mouth with his.

"What—"

"Your turn," he smiled against her mouth, then scooped her up in his arms and carried her across the room, to where the stove fire warmed the sofa, and lay her back against the cushions, planting a hand on her chest as he knelt between her legs and tilted her hips up to meet his mouth.

All thoughts fled under the onslaught of his full lips and insistent tongue. Her desire already honed to a fine point by their earlier activities, it wasn't long before she was writhing on the couch, reaching for him. His hand on her chest had her trapped though, and she rested her feet on his shoulder blades, clawing at the cushions of the couch in sweet agony.

The very moment that she came, crying out his name in ecstasy, he rose up before her, covering her body with his own and sliding inside her to the hilt.

"See what you do to me," he rasped into her ear. "I'm ready for you again." And then he began to thrust, and Ivy couldn't form words.

It was impossible, but he was bringing her there again, a cascade of orgasms that shuddered through her one after the other. She could barely move, just lie there and feel as he drove into her, over and over. Archer held her head in his hands, cradling her carefully as he whispered half-heard oaths in her ears, rutting against her with quick urgent, movements.

The light from the fire flickered behind her eyelids like it was midsummer, and they lay in the leaves of the forest with drums all around them and lust in the air. And with every thrust, she heard his thoughts, echoing inside her like they were her own.

You're mine, Ivy Potter. Tonight, you are mine. No matter what happens, I have this moment.

Ivy struggled to turn her face to his, but the way he was lying, crushing her into the sofa, she could only see his temple, the curls of his wild hair. She moved her lips against his ear.

"I love you, Archer."

Hear me. I love you.

All at once, Archer went rigid against her, and everything crashed, tumbling, endless, and she clung to him like they were the single, bright spot in a universe gone dark.

I love you, Ivy. I love you love you love you…

As the throbbing of their orgasms subsided, Archer slumped against her, panting. She caressed his shoulders and back, lost in her dreamy pleasure state.

Until suddenly he pulled away. Sprang away, really, like some frightened creature.

Ivy sat up, confused, cold, and missing his touch. Archer stood, naked, staring at her in abject horror.

She grabbed a throw blanket to cover her nakedness and looked up at him. "Archer?"

He gave a small, nearly imperceptible shake of his head. "No. Oh please, no."

"What's wrong?" She reached for him, and that's when she saw it. Her left hand. Two of her fingers, thumb, and wrist were riddled with dark veins like winter twigs, branching outward as if ready to pop through her skin.

She gasped and held her hand away from her. "What is it? What do I do?"

"Sweet Ivy." He squeezed his eyes shut. "I didn't know."

She ran for the sink and turned the taps to scalding, but all the scrubbing in the world didn't make the marks vanish. Her hand seemed to tingle beneath her touch, pulsing with her heartbeat, and the markings grew thicker, a pressure building up beneath her fingertips. The veins were traveling up her arm now, nearly to her elbow.

The bramble tree rose up in her mind's eye, its pulsing, terrible shapes. "Get it off, get it off," she begged, and washed harder.

A hand clamped down on her shoulder and whirled her around. Archer was wearing pants again, and his forest boots, but his eyes were intent on her arm. He ran his fingers over the markings, muttering under his breath.

"No choice…" He gripped her hard.

Ice seemed to flow through her veins, stopping her heart, freezing her thoughts. She stood as if frozen as Archer concentrated on her arm, his body quaking. After a moment, he doubled over with pain, gasping, and let her go. She recoiled, slumped against the counter, and stared at him.

He turned away.

Her tongue seemed too full for her mouth and she focused on moving air into her lungs. In. Out. In. Out. "Archer."

He straightened, and walked toward the door.

She followed. "Wait. Tell me, what was that?"

He said nothing as he grabbed the door handle and pulled it open. By the time he hit the porch, he was running.

"Stop!" she cried, and held out her hand—her flawless, creamy hand.

He looked back at her once, his black eyes awash in pain, then lifted his arms.

A hedge of brambles exploded from her floorboards, blocking her in.

"No!" she screamed, and ran back inside. The windows...

But Archer was too quick, and vines and twigs bloomed over every window, blocking out the sight of the snow, the street, and the pale figure of her lover, disappearing into the night.

~

It was the sound of chainsaws that woke her, long after the wood stove had gone cherry-dim, long after she'd cried her insides out and gone to sleep in her darkened, wood-encased shop.

She blinked, and drew her blanket close around her. She was still naked, still scented with sex, her hair wild about her shoulders, and there was a buzz of electricity and the whine of metal teeth biting through brambles just beyond the door.

She jumped to her feet, looking around the shop.

"Help!" she said, though what she thought was, *Wait!*

"Ivy Potter!" It was the voice of Ernest Beemer. "Are you all right?"

She ran to her room and grabbed her bathrobe, wrapping it tight around her and tying the knot. The movements seemed so simple, her hands almost automatic, and she blinked down at them in wonder. They shouldn't be able to do that. To just work, like human hands. Like normal hands.

These hands, that had driven Archer away.

She checked her reflection in the mirror quickly, but found nothing amiss. Her eyes were the same color as always, her hair just hair, not brambles or violets or fire.

Her eyes burned and her chest squeezed and Archer, damn it all, had run away from her again.

"I'm here," she called, through the lump in her throat. "I'm fine. What… what happened?" she added weakly, as if playing innocent might fly.

"It looks like your house was attacked in the night," came the reply through the hedge of thorns. The chainsaw started up again.

It looked like she had some time. Trapper was lying on the towels, watching her with careful eyes. Some time, during the long, desperate night, she'd given him more pain medication and changed his bandages, spreading out some newspaper next to his

162

bed, in case he needed it. The dog still seemed out of it, probably wondering where he was and why it hurt to move.

Ivy knew the feeling.

In the bathroom, she ran a cloth under the taps and washed, shivering at the ice-cold water but not wanting to take the time to wait until it heated up. A quick brush with a comb and she grabbed a fresh set of long underwear and a bra, shoved her legs into slacks and her arms into her last clean sweater. Socks, boots, hat. Check. Costumed in normalcy, she headed out to the front, just in time to see the first rays of light break through the brambles that blocked her front door.

Soon enough, there was a person-sized hole carved into the hedge, and hands reaching for her to help her out into the morning sunlight.

It was later than she'd thought, locked away inside the nest of thorns. Mid-morning sunlight washed over the street, turning the snow into a field of glittering diamonds. Her house was half-encased in browning vines, stiff and dying against the windows and doors. When she looked back at the biggest hedge, there before her front door, it too, seemed to be dying, crumbling and rotting before their eyes.

"Whatever this was, it doesn't have much staying power," said Beemer, pulling at one of the branches. It broke off in his hand. "It's dead. Just like in the greenhouse."

"The greenhouse?" Ivy turned to look at the men around her in turn but no one seemed in the mood to answer her questions, and her patience had run out.

She headed around the back of the shop herself, and as soon as the dome came into view, she broke into a run.

The windows and metal veins were black, crusted over with some strange residue. The broken-in door lay open, the wrought iron gate torn away and thrown aside. But the brambles that had so recently blocked the door were gone, and the floor and walls were coated in char and ash. Ivy approached the threshold, heart in her throat.

The black trails ran along the floor inside, coating every pane of glass with smears of ash, but every trace of the bramble-tree was gone. She walked the paths of the greenhouse floor, half fearing, and half already sure of what she'd see.

The redbell patch came into view— or rather, what had once been redbell. The square of ground was picked clean, and the tree that had sprung up in the spot was burned to the root, a twisting, hulking chunk of crumbling charcoal. Archer's effect on this place had been burned away, and the redbells he'd come for were long gone.

So Archer must be, too.

Ivy dropped to her knees in the dirt, surveying the destruction around her. How much dark magic must it have taken to destroy the bramble bush here, if removing the marks on her hand had been enough to turn his eyes black last night? And if he'd been coursing with so much darkness, how had he ever gotten the flowers back into the forest unharmed?

Unless, caught in the thrall of so much evil magic, he'd destroyed them, too.

These days, I go quickly to curses.

She bowed her head over her knees and let out a quaking breath. There had been moments last night that she'd thought she'd been close. But he'd warned her, hadn't he?

The magic… it's broken something inside me.

And looking around the wreck of her greenhouse, Ivy realized that whatever was broken, it might not be something she could fix.

Dimly, she became aware of footsteps behind her, and she scraped the back of her hand across her eyes and sniffed. *Keep it together, Ivy, or everyone will know you aren't just crying over a few panes of glass.*

"It is a relief, is it not, that the enchantments were short-lived?" The voice of Deacon Ryder wafted through the chilled air. "Even if you now have this mess to deal with."

"A bit of soap and water," she said, keeping her tone even. "We'll be fine."

"Really?" the deacon toed a shredded redbell stalk. "But what of your customers and the headaches they claim to have? When the bells start to ring again, they'll be wanting their redbell tea."

She took a sharp breath. *Claim?* Those headaches had nearly killed her. And now that she understood fully what part her father had in creating the barrier, she understood that it wasn't only love driving his obsession to develop the redbell tea for her and their neighbors—it was guilt.

Though she still wasn't sure if she believed the deacon's story. Everything he said was so twisted. Didn't she know her father better than that? He'd been wary of Archer, but that was because he hadn't wanted Ivy to be hurt, same as he'd been hurt when her mother had left them.

Although, maybe she hadn't known her father as well as she thought. Perhaps he was far more heartbroken than her child's sensibilities had ever been able to comprehend. Those long hours she'd spent last night, trapped away in her house after Archer had left—that had been her father's whole life. He'd never let her know, protecting her own, distant relationship with her mother, her own fantasy about her parents.

And then, when she and Archer had fallen in love, George Potter had let his fear and heartbreak ruin everything. What a wretched kind of love, to be so soaked in fear. A fear that could kill forests and children, that could divide people from each other and themselves.

Ivy would never love like that. And she'd never live like that again.

"And I suppose," the deacon was saying now, though Ivy was only listening with half an ear, "that you now see the need for us to protect ourselves. This attack on your home is proof enough that the forest knows how important you are to our cause."

She stood, dusting her hands off. Enough was enough. There was a reason Archer had locked her in her house last night—he knew that if she came after him, he wouldn't be able to stop her. Ivy had a job to do, and it was in the forest.

She turned sharply on her heel and strode to the door, and the deacon, taken aback, followed behind her.

"Ivy, you must not let all your father's work be in vain. We need you to help us resurrect the barrier."

At the door she turned to look at him. "Are you kidding? No. I will not lift a finger to help you with the bells. They have been a source of constant torture to me for the past three years. They killed my father and my mother."

He blinked at her. "Your forest folk mother? How do you know that? Ivy, have you been in contact with the forest folk? What do you know of the barrier's destruction—" He reached for her hand, but she shook him off and walked on, mentally preparing a checklist in her mind. She'd need food. A heavy coat. Water. Probably a hunting knife, just to be safe. Her father's pack should be in his closet...

"Listen, young lady," Deacon Ryder said, scurrying behind her as she headed up the front porch. "You're too young to fully understand the implications of your decision. This town is in grave danger. *You* are in grave danger."

The hedge was crumbling away before their eyes now, rotting like old wood. "This doesn't look dangerous to me. This looks like some half-hearted effort to trap me inside my house. My father did the exact same thing to me on the night the bells began, only he used a metal lock."

And Ivy wasn't a child anymore. She shook her head and slipped inside. Pack. Water. Food.

The deacon scrambled in behind her, uninvited. "Your father was trying to protect you!"

Archer was trying to protect her, too. From himself. But what her father and Archer didn't realize was that their efforts only isolated her. For three years, she'd believed in her father's choices. She'd

167

stayed in her little shop, brewing her little teas, and not taking any chances. She'd trusted that others knew better than she what it was she needed.

No longer.

She filled a canteen with water and grabbed some nuts from the pantry.

"What are you doing?"

She brushed by him and retrieved her father's old hiking backpack from his room, stuffing some spare clothes, water, food and other necessities inside. She zipped up her coat, hoisted the pack on her shoulders, and clipped the waistband.

"Oh, no you don't." He stepped in front of her, blocking her path to the door.

From far across the room, she heard a rumble. Trapper pushed himself up on his paws and growled.

"Deacon," she said, "I believe your dog has missed you." Then she darted around him and headed out into the sunlight.

eighteen

ACROSS THE STREET, there were men clustered around the barrier at the place Archer had broken through.

"Excuse me, gentlemen," Ivy said, as she approached the crowd. Everyone was talking at once, a frantic flurry of fear.

"Several yards of the lattice is missing—"

"—Whatever came through here burnt these wires to a crisp."

"Ask Beemer. We need to get this prepared by tonight or it'll do us no good—"

Ivy pushed her way through to the gap in the barrier, mentally reviewing her map of the forest. It would take about half an hour to reach the village, provided it was in the same place as it had been when Ivy was a teen. Up close, she could see there was indeed a huge gap in the barrier, a hole nearly as wide as a truck, as if a fireball had barreled through the lattice, singeing the metal and bells along the edges.

She swallowed. This hadn't been how Archer had first come through — after breaking the enchantments, there had been a tiny tear in the lattice, barely enough for his body.

"There she is," Ernest Beemer was saying, turning her way. "Miss Potter, has the deacon spoken to you about what is required?"

All eyes were on her now. And though she'd been brave enough when arguing with the deacon, the thought of announcing her intentions to this mob made her blood run cold. Still, her decision had been made. There was no point in keeping it a secret.

"I will not help you raise the barrier," she said, standing straight. "It is damaging to both the forest and to my neighbors on either side. The last time the barrier went up, we all suffered horrible headaches, and the side effects for the forest folk was doubtless doubly bad."

"How do you know?" someone called.

"I knew it," said Shawn. "She's in collusion with them."

Ivy held up a hand. "The only remedy was the redbell tea, but my redbell crop has been destroyed. We cannot raise the barrier or I and all of my customers—townsfolk just like you—will suffer. Now, excuse me. I'm going into the forest."

A wall of men materialized before her.

"You're not going anywhere," Beemer said. "This entire town is in danger because of that damn forest, and you're whining about a couple of headaches?"

Ivy cast her eyes around the crowd, hoping to find the face of at least one of her customers. Where was Jeb this morning? Where was Sallie?

"Please let me go." Was that a note of begging in her voice? That would never do.

"Hell, no," said Shawn. He grabbed her arm. "We have no idea what you're going into the forest to do."

She tried to wrench her arm away but Shawn's grip was tight. "At the very least, I'm going to warn the forest folk—what's left of them—that you plan to raise the barrier again. This time, I intend to give them a chance to escape."

"Into our town?" Beemer exploded. "Are you crazy? That's exactly the kind of element we don't need. Magic-wielding forest folk? How is that supposed to keep us safe?"

She turned on him. "How is shutting people in a forest you claim is overrun with dark magic supposed to keep anyone safe?" She pointed with her free hand into the woods. "There are children dying in there, Mr. Beemer. Dying because of the bells."

There was a murmur in the crowd and she looked around at the brothers, husbands, fathers standing there, looking skeptical.

"Stop her!" came a shout. "Stop Ivy Potter before she gets into the forest!" The deacon was running up from Petal & Leaf.

"Don't worry, deacon," Shawn drawled. "She's not going anywhere."

"Ivy," Deacon Ryder panted. "I'm sorry, child, but we have no choice." He looked at Shawn. "Put her in the van."

Shawn nodded and pulled her out of the crowd, jerking roughly on her arm. Ivy dug her heels in as he yanked her down the street to a waiting van. He opened the rear door and shoved her inside, unceremoniously slamming it behind her.

Ivy pushed herself to her feet, blinking in the dim light. There were several other people inside, sitting listlessly around the floor of the van. Every one was a customer of Petal & Leaf.

"Good morning, Ivy," said Jeb.

Sallie waved. "Did you bring any food?"

~

Hours passed in the dark, chilly van, and despite shifting positions multiple times, Ivy's butt began to hurt from the cold, metal floors. She'd long ago split her water and trail mix with the other prisoners, and they'd tried, and failed, to use her hunting knife to pry open the doors or the grill that separated them from the driver's seat.

Jeb had asked her about the pack, first thing, and Ivy didn't see much reason to hide the truth from any of them. She told them about Archer breaking the enchantment on the bells, and how he'd used dark magic to do it. She told them how he'd come to her for help with the redbell medicine, and how he wasn't particularly good at controlling the evil he conjured.

She kept the more salacious details to herself.

"Dark magic's a pernicious beast," Jeb observed. "And Archer doesn't seem like he has the spirit for it."

"Archer's plenty spirited!" argued Sallie. She winked at Ivy. "*You* know."

But Jeb was not deterred. "He's not a ranger, not a warrior. Of that world but in love with another. Like your father, Ivy, only the other way 'round."

"You wouldn't know it to see him now," Ivy said, as a shiver stole across her skin. There were three other forest-blooded people in the van — Bette and her two grandchildren, Rowan and Rose. Their father worked in the lumberyards a hundred miles south, and must be on duty this weekend. The twins were sleeping on their grandmother's legs, and she was casting fearful looks at Ivy and the others while pretending to knit.

How nice of their captors to let them bring knitting.

"Dark magic does something to a body," Jeb went on. "You're never quite the same after."

Ivy hugged her knees to her chest. Her father certainly had never been the same once he'd helped cast the enchantments on the barrier bells. And Archer was infinitely more powerful, and had done far worse. Perhaps she was naive to think there was any hope of getting to him at all.

"What are we going to do?" Bette asked. "They're going to put those bells up again? My son will surely make us move away now."

"We might all have to move away," said Sallie. "Ivy says her crop of redbell's gone. When those forsaken bells start to ring, we're all in trouble."

"They won't be able to raise the barrier again." Ivy's voice was firm. "It requires enchantments they don't possess."

"What do you mean?" Jeb asked.

Ivy took a deep breath. "My father... he helped them with the barrier spell all those years ago."

"No! Ivy..." Sallie looked disapproving, as if Ivy were a child telling falsehoods. She only wished it were so easy.

"Yes." She had to get it out. "He helped Beemer and Ryder cast the spell, though that's not what either of them call it. The deacon calls it a miracle. Archer says it's dark magic."

"Ought to be," murmured Jeb darkly, "if it took three."

"But my father's gone," she pointed out. "So they can't get the bells going again."

"Then why do they have us in here?" Sallie asked.

Ivy looked at her. "Well, I was trying to go into the forest. Weren't you?"

Sallie chuckled. "No, child. I was tearing the lattice off every tree limb."

"The children were pulling down the silent bells," Bette volunteered.

"I was already in the forest, trying to salvage some of the dead trees," admitted Jeb.

The driver's side door opened, and Shawn climbed into the seat.

"You let us out of here, Shawn Cooper," Sallie cried.

Shawn put on his seatbelt and faced front. "Quiet down back there. I don't want this to get ugly."

"It already is ugly!" Jeb banged on the grate keeping them separated. "You can't keep us prisoner here!"

"You're disrupting the peace and breaking town ordinances about going into the forest," Shawn replied.

"So call the cops," Jeb snapped.

Shawn said nothing, just shifted the van into gear and began to drive.

They drove straight along the forest's edge for quite some time, and Jeb peppered Shawn with questions the younger man refused to answer.

"Where are you taking us? Do you know what the punishment is for kidnapping? For kidnapping *children*? I'll have you arrested for this, Shawn, I swear I will!"

But Ivy doubted that. All five cops on the force were dyed-in-the-wool townsfolk, completely in support of the bells.

After a bit, Shawn veered left, and the wheels went from old asphalt to gravel.

"We're at the quarry," Bette said, as the children blinked awake.

The quarry cut into the giant cliff that marked the edge of town and the edge of the forest. Here the bell lattice was driven deep into the rock, affixed with gigantic metal bolts and springs, like something you might see at a power station.

"If I had magic like my pa did," Jeb mumbled, "we'd be fine."

But none of them had any magic. Ivy nodded mutely. They were trapped—trapped like the forest folk, by the bigots in this town. Looking at Jeb, the way his hands lay fisted on the metal floor, she could understand why even someone as gentle and lighthearted as Archer might have turned to dark magic. It was a terrible feeling, to be trapped.

At last Shawn shut off the engine and got out, leaving them there again.

"Nana?" asked Rose. "I need to go potty."

"There, there, child," Bette stroked the little girl's head. "Soon."

Ivy took in a breath and let it out. They'd have to release them eventually…right?

She didn't want to think about why they'd been driven all the way to the quarry. A few more minutes passed in silence and then they started to hear voices and footsteps shuffling in the gravel outside.

"What are they saying?" Sallie asked.

But none of them had forest ears, so they couldn't tell.

At last, the door to the van opened, revealing an overcast sky, and the beginnings of twilight.

"Ivy Potter," said the voice of Deacon Ryder. "Get out."

She unfolded her cramped legs and slid to the ground. As she straightened, she saw a crowd of townsfolk looking on her with nervous eyes, and remembered the meetings in the square, the whispers of "forest-lover" and the suspicious glares.

"We're here to raise the barrier again tonight, and your town needs your help. A terrible evil will overtake us if we don't divide ourselves from the forest. You must agree."

She shook her head. "I don't. And you can lock me up in this van all night and day and I'll still never agree with you. The barrier made me sick. It made a lot of people in this town sick. And it hurt and killed the forest, and the folk inside. I don't know what it is you think you're protecting us from, but it's not worth the price we pay."

As she heard Archer's words fall from her lips, Ivy felt a sob rise in her throat. How long had she just obeyed the status quo? Her father had helped raise the barrier, so she tolerated it, let it make her and her friends sick, listened to its incessant jangling, built her whole life around managing the side effects, instead of fighting for the real cure. Archer may have turned to darkness, but he destroyed the bells. She should have done the same.

"Don't listen to her," cried a voice in the crowd. "She's half forest-folk anyway."

"Witch," cried another. Some held flashlights or lanterns up against the growing darkness. She couldn't see their faces, though their voices sounded familiar.

Perhaps Jeb had been right. She'd never been a townie at all.

"I'm sorry to hear that," said the Deacon, and indeed, he sounded devastated.

Oh well, she wanted to snap back at him. Guess my soul is lost for all eternity. Strange, though. It felt like the opposite. She felt as though she could fly.

"What should we do?" Beemer was asking Ryder. "You're the spirit, and I'm the body…"

"But the miracle won't work without the heart."

"So that's the spell," she spat at him. "Spirit, body, heart? And blood to bind it all? Be honest with yourself, Deacon. You're doing dark magic." She raised her voice. "Do you know that? This barrier which you think protects the town from magic is stronger than most of the enchantments in the forest!"

Stronger than any she'd seen, in fact, except Archer's. He'd been even stronger, to be able to break it.

There was a rumble through the crowd, and Beemer hissed and shook his head. "Enough of this. I'm not going to lose any more time or money to these backwards customs. Grab her."

Hands clamped down on her arms and shoulders and Shawn jerked her hand out toward Beemer, who approached with a cup and something flashing silver in the lantern light. A knife.

"Let go!" she screamed, wide-eyed, looking to the crowd around her. Why was everyone just standing there while she was being attacked? "Help me!"

Nothing.

Deacon Ryder hovered behind, wringing his hands. "This isn't ideal. It's supposed to be of one's own free will."

"Superstitions," Beemer grumbled. "Blood is blood." And then he sliced into Ivy's hand.

She gasped, but the pain wasn't really so bad. She'd cut herself worse on shears in the greenhouse. It was the shock, the utter violation, and the fact that there were all these people standing around, waiting for it to happen. This was supposed to be *her* town.

Beemer caught some blood in the cup, then stood back. "That should do it. Let's get a move on."

Ivy whimpered as her blood dripped onto the gravel. Shawn still held her firmly as Mr. Beemer and Deacon Ryder headed over to one of the large, metal-grid elevators that ran up the side of the cliff and ascended.

As soon as they were gone, Shawn dropped her to the ground, and Ivy cradled her hand to her chest.

"What the hell is wrong with you?!" she shouted at him.

"Why can't you just do as you're told?" he shot back. He turned toward the back of the van. "Out, all of you."

Jeb, Sallie, Bette, and the children wasted no time scrambling out of the back of the vehicle. Jeb carried Ivy's pack.

"You can't cause any more problems now," Shawn said.

"You're a monster," Bette said.

"You forest people would know," he snapped.

Jeb rushed over to Ivy. "Let me look at your hand."

"There's a First Aid kit in my pack." As Jeb cleaned the wound on her palm and wrapped her hand in a bandage, Ivy looked up at the elevator, high at the top of the cliff. "What are they doing up there?"

"Black magic," he said. "Blood magic."

"I don't know much about that."

"Good girl."

No, it wasn't good. If she knew dark magic, maybe she'd know how to stop it. If she knew what held this town and Archer in its grip, she'd be able to fight it.

Jeb finished up with the bandages then straightened to look at the crowd. "This whole town is cursed tonight. You made a mistake once, three years ago, out of fear and ignorance. But tonight you have assaulted your neighbors. You have kidnapped children!"

Some of the people looked guilty at that accusation, but one of the townies called out, "You hate it here so much, you should just leave. Go back to the forest."

"That's how I found myself in the back of this fine gentleman's van."

Ivy shook her head. What was the use? The bells would start to ring again and this time, they didn't even have redbell. She shut her eyes and sighed. This was what Archer had said would happen, wasn't it? That's why he wanted to take the redbell and escape back into the forest with it. He knew that no one in the town would listen long enough to realize they had nothing to fear.

A twang traveled down the length of the lattice, shivering all the thousands of tiny, silver bells like the first lance of a migraine.

Sallie, Jeb, and Ivy put their hands over their ears, but after that one little clang, they stopped again. Ivy looked around. Bette, wisely, seem to have disappeared with the children. Thank goodness. No one needed to be here to see this abomination. If she were Bette, she'd be running with the kids out of town.

"I can't go to the forest," Sallie was saying, a sob catching her throat. "I don't know anyone there. My pa's long dead, and I was never close to my forest side." She looked up at the lattice, her eyes wide. "But I can't take those bells. Not without the tea. I can't take it."

Jeb put his arm around her. "We'll figure something out."

Ivy didn't know what. Perhaps they'd leave town entirely, start somewhere new. Maybe this was the perfect solution for the townsfolk, not only to divide themselves from the forest, but to cast out any remaining citizens with links to the land. Ivy tried to imagine going back to her old life, and couldn't. She tried to imagine leaving, like her fantasy of escape the night the bells stopped, but found she couldn't picture that either. There was no life for her out in the world, in desert or city or tropical island. She peered into the endless forest. Archer was in there. Her Archer. And he needed her.

Over the winter wind, she thought she heard the sound of music. Something pale flashed between the trees.

Around her, the people seemed to notice it, too. Some turned their flashlights on the woods, as the night turned lavender and blue and black. The noise got louder—not the clanging din of silver bells, but soft, sweet melodies. Songs Ivy remembered from summers in the trees.

A moment later, the first child stepped out of the forest.

nineteen

HER REDDISH HAIR WAS BRAIDED in a crown about her head, and a redbell was tucked behind one ear. She looked a bit like Archer, and Ivy recognized her at once. A black-haired boy came next, in a brown hide coat, with redbell in his buttonhole. More children followed, each in their simple forest clothes and each sporting a single, crimson flower. All were singing.

"It's the forest folk." The whisper traveled through the group like a wave.

There were more than a dozen now, more than two dozen, and their parents followed, their hands outstretched, their skin and clothes pale as deer bellies in the darkness.

"They'll bewitch us!" someone cried.

They approached, walking right up to the border of silent bells. A young woman came to stand with the first two children. Her hair fell like a midnight waterfall down her back and her face was one Ivy had seen in Archer's visions. She stood and went over to the woman.

"I am River," she said to Ivy. "Thank you for the flowers."

"Archer's sister-in-law?" Ivy asked.

The woman cocked her head to the side. "It is not your townie law that made him my family, but yes."

"What are you doing here?" Shawn yelled from what he must have considered a safe distance.

"We were told they plan to resurrect the barrier."

"Told by Archer?" Ivy asked.

The woman nodded, sadly. "It was a great sacrifice for him. We have come to escape the forest, while there is still time. It is no longer a place for us, but we will use your gift of redbell to provide us with safe passage through your town into a new wilderness."

Of course. They hadn't wanted the redbell to help them survive in the forest, but rather to help them survive outside of it.

Another twang of the lattice, and the dozens of forest folk joined Ivy and her friends in crouching and wincing in pain.

"We'd better do this quick," said Jeb, and yanked at the bottom of the barrier, trying to create a gap for the forest folk to slip through.

"Wait, stop!" cried Shawn and he started to step forward, but another townie placed a hand on his arm.

"They want to be free from the forest," she argued. "These children, they want to be free. We have to help them."

River nodded. "We will die trapped away in here. We have no choice."

Shawn turned on the townsfolk. "You want them in your town?"

"They won't be in the town, moron," Ivy said. "None of us can live here when the barrier goes up." She wasn't sure where else the forest folk could go, though. They were sensitive to the trappings of civilization, to electricity and steel and cell phone towers. But that would be a problem they solved later, out of earshot of the deadly bells.

Ivy searched the group in the forest. "Where is Archer?"

River looked at her curiously. "He isn't one of us."

"He's choosing to stay in the forest?" she asked. "Alone?"

The woman was unfazed, and her voice was calm when she replied. "He has been alone, Ivy Potter. You cannot wield such dark magics and live among people." Then she turned to crawl beneath the barrier after her children.

As Jeb and Sallie helped the forest folk to crawl through the gap between the lattice and the ground, River turned to Ivy and pointed up the cliff.

"How many of them are casting this spell?"

"Two," Ivy replied.

"Two? A strange number for black magic."

"It's the blood of three," Jeb corrected, still pulling kids out. "They stole some of Ivy's blood when she wouldn't help them."

"My father," Ivy explained. "He did the spell with them the first time." Then she remembered what Ernest Beemer said when he'd cut her. "Something about the two other men being spirit and body, and my father—and me—being the heart."

"Blood magics," River confirmed. "They'll need three, and midnight. We have a few hours yet, to get away."

"But what about Archer?" Ivy begged River. "He can't stay in the forest alone. He'll be consumed."

"He's lost," River replied, her tone so detached Ivy's fingers itched to slap her. "He's been lost since the moment he agreed to try to stop the bells. Just like his brother. They gave their souls to help us."

"No!" Ivy said. "I saw him!"

River looked at her sadly. "You do not see much, Ivy Potter, with your townie eyes."

"I saw all I needed," Ivy snapped. Who did this lady think she was, the queen of the forest? "Yes, he does dark magic, but he did it for you. You can't leave him alone in the forest. With nothing to fight for, how will there be any chance of saving him?"

"There *is* no chance of saving him," said River. "He has helped us, but he hasn't triumphed. Archer is lost, Ivy Potter. Trust me. I know more of magic than you."

Ivy grit her teeth. That may be true, but she knew more of Archer than anyone. She'd let him go once, and his own people had allowed him to sacrifice himself. Ivy may not be forest folk, but she belonged to Archer, and he to her. She wasn't letting him get stuck in the forest again.

A third shudder traveled down the wires, scorching through their eardrums. Jeb hissed and dropped the lattice on a forest woman, who screamed in agony. As they pulled her out from beneath the barrier, great red lacerations appeared on her flesh, as

185

if she'd been cut with a whip. Jeb looked down at his hands, which bore similar markings.

Ivy turned to retrieve her First Aid kit.

Suddenly, a few of the townsfolk stepped up. "Grab that over there," said one to another, "let's get these people out quick."

The woman who'd argued with Shawn looked at her. "They won't hurt us yet, right? Just the magic people?"

Ivy nodded mutely.

River stared up at the cliffs. "It is a strong spell they are casting, and a ruthless one. Three legs form a steady stool. The body man and spirit man, they must have firm beliefs."

Ivy knew they did. Deacon Ryder truly believed the forest was evil, and the forest folk devils out to steal all their souls. And Ernest was in it for the money for his quarry— the dangers of the forest kept big business from town and material wealth from his pockets.

"Heart — that is your blood?"

"Yes," Ivy said. "Because my father. He… loved me, and he was afraid he'd lose me to the forest."

River's eyes widened, but she said nothing, which was fine by Ivy. She didn't need anyone else to pity her father, and his wretched, fearful love.

The last of the forest folk were crawling under the gap. Ivy stared out into the darkness.

"Where is he?" she asked softly.

River hesitated. "My man is gone, too, Ivy Potter. My children's father."

Ivy nodded. "Archer told me. He died taking on the barrier."

"Long before that, he was taken by dark magic. I know how it feels to lose him."

She bit her lip. "Archer's not dead."

River took a deep breath. "He wants to be. The darkness is too extreme. Let him go."

"No!" The word tore out of her. "I will never let him go."

Behind her, the forest folk were gathering, readying to set off into the unknown. Ivy looked down at the space where they'd all crawled through.

"Ivy," Jeb warned. "You cannot go into the forest."

She turned to River. "Tell me where to find him. I know you know."

River was silent, studying Ivy, her modern clothes and her townie features. "I do not. But when he brought the flowers, wrapped in your greenhouse moss, he also had with him a knot of the bell lattice. I believe he has made his choice."

Ivy chest felt tight, remembering the giant hole in the lattice right across from her shop. The one they'd been repairing when Shawn had thrown her in the van. "His choice?"

"Yes," said River. "Like his brother, Archer will die when the bells begin to ring."

~

"Are you sure you know what you're doing, Ivy-girl?" Jeb asked her when she slipped beneath the barrier.

No. Of course not. Ivy didn't have the slightest clue what she was doing. She could not search the entire forest in a few hours, and she wasn't entirely

187

sure if she could even get to Archer once she'd found him.

But she had to try.

"I'm going to get Archer," was all she said. "I'm going to get him."

"But what about the bells?" Jeb asked. "You'll be trapped in the forest."

She nodded. "I know. But I spent three years trapped on this side. It's time to try something new."

It was crazy how convincing she sounded.

"Good luck." He waved.

Ivy tried not to cry as she took off into the woods.

First she made a beeline down the barrier toward her shop, searching for a hint of silver lattice work in the ground. If Archer planned to commit suicide by bell, he'd have to attach the bells he stole to the rest of the lattice somehow. Right?

It wasn't much of a plan, but it was all she had.

She hurried through the deadened trees at the edge of the forest, sloughing through fallen leaves and hopping over roots and rocks. There was no sound in the forest tonight—even if any fauna had come closer to the bells during these last two days of silence, they were clearly wiser than Ivy, and had fled at the first tingle of the barrier bells. Though she hadn't been in the forest in years, she had never heard such total silence, on either side of the barrier.

Every time the bells rang out, a fresh wave of pain sent her into a cowering crouch, covering her ears and crying out in pain. Her jaw ached from gritting her teeth, her stomach roiled with nausea, and a slow, pounding agony took up residence inside her skull. The sound was coming more often now, every ten minutes, then every five, then every three. She wasn't sure how much longer she had—how much longer *Archer* had.

The first question she'd won from him in the game, his story of coming for her the morning after the bells started to ring, loomed large in her mind.

They filled the air, setting everything on fire. The trees, the soil. But I kept walking. My blood boiled beneath my skin. My face blistered, my bones crumbled. And still I walked.

Ivy didn't walk. She ran, and in her head, larger than the pain, louder than the bells, stood Archer, her own, lovely Archer, who she'd thought she'd lost, and who she never wanted to lose again.

There! A line of silver, a single wire running from the main barrier lattice into the heart of the forest. She stopped to peer through the bells, trying to get her bearings. They were just down the street from Petal and Leaf.

All of a sudden, Ivy knew exactly where Archer had gone.

She sprinted into the forest, heedless of dead trees and beasties. The woods were rotted and black, like ghosts from a forest fire, and she leaped over downed limbs and piles of char. Three horrible rings of the bells later, she saw it, a great, ancient tree rising up from the forest floor, blackened to a crisp, but still standing. And there, in the side of the bark, was affixed a row of rungs reaching high into the canopy.

Don't be afraid, Ivy-mine, Archer had whispered into her ear on that warm, summer night. *Climb up. I'll see you at the top.*

The silver thread also wound its way up the trunk. Ivy squeezed her eyes shut.

Damn you, Archer.

The splintered rungs were hell on her injured hand, and slippery with ice and snow. Her feet broke off chunks of rotted wood with every step, and each ring of the bells—faster now, every two minutes, every one— sent shockwaves of pain and nausea through her body. It had been nearly three days since she'd drunk redbell tea. Even if she made it to him, the barrier might kill her.

But he'd come looking for her the day the bells started to ring. They'd nearly killed him, but he kept on. And so would she. For if he'd chosen this tree, of all the trees in the forest, it meant he was hers, still.

He was hers, and she wasn't letting him go.

Ivy's fingers were raw and bleeding by the time she reached the platform Archer had built in the branches. The flowers were long gone, of course, nothing but crackling vines on blackened boughs, an empty ruin swaying in a deadened tree. It was nearly midnight in deep winter, and there was no one up here.

The bells sounded again and she collapsed on the platform, huddled into a ball, covering her head with her hands, her mouth open in a silent scream. Midnight was nearly upon her now, and with it, death and enchantment. And Archer wasn't here at all.

A flash of silver drew her eye as the bells tapered off, but no—it was just a knot of bells and wire, wrapped tight around a mess of branches.

A sob escaped her throat. Was it one last, cruel trick, to think that she might find him in their bower?

"So," croaked the branches, in a voice like low thunder. "You are an angel, after all."

"Archer!" She crawled over to him. He looked like part of the tree, charred and crumbly, with black

190

smoke pouring off of him like he'd just been taken from a fire. There were angry red lines where the silver wire cut into his shoulders and neck and wrists, and his features were barely discernible in the deep night. "I've come to get you."

"Archer is gone," he said. "You cannot fuck him out of me anymore."

"Shut up!" She hadn't come to argue with the darkness, but to fight it.

The bells rang again. He let out a cry of pain and she wavered, woozy, while blackness crowded the edges of her vision.

When the bells silenced, she reached out and began unwinding the wires from his skin.

"Stop," he said, unmoving. "I will kill you if I'm free."

"Not before the bells do," Ivy said. "And I think one of us, at least, should survive this."

"Don't you see?" he asked, as she finished with his arms and started in on the loops around his neck. "I do not want to live like this, in this endless darkness I've made for myself. I do not want to live without you."

"Then help me get you out of here," she said, leaning in between his spread legs to tug at the wires. "And we'll run away from the bells, and we'll figure out the whole black magic thing some other time."

The bells jangled again, and Ivy gasped as they singed her fingers.

Archer's voice was scary and calm. "You make it sound so simple."

"It *is* simple," she insisted. There was a knot there, high on his neck, and she realized she should have brought wire cutters. "Listen to me: I love you. I

191

love you more than all the dark magic in the world, and I am not afraid."

From far away, there was a sound—a clamorous earthquake, a crystalline train crash, the horrid, deathly jingle of a million, million bells. The enchantment was complete.

Ivy reached for Archer again, but it was all too quick. The wires lit up in her hands, the silver shone like starlight, and the bells everywhere began to ring.

Then, all at once, the sound resolved, the discordance smoothed, shifting into a harmony, a molten-golden tone that fell onto Ivy's ears like the sweetest redbell tea, like the softest summer morning, like the whisper of a loved one. Out from her hands, the golden glow spread, dancing down the lines and lighting up the bells like tiny suns.

And where those bells touched Archer, the darkness melted away. His skin shone through the burns, his hair shifted back to red, and at last, his eyes cleared, moss-green and smiling up at her like they had every time in this tree.

I love you, and I am not afraid.

How foolish the townfolk had been to use Ivy for their spell. Her belief was strong, but it wasn't the one they wanted. She may have been her father's daughter, but her love was not made weak by fear. It was powerful, and true, and more than any black magic could bear.

Ivy's hands dropped to her sides. "Archer…"

He lifted them to his lips, kissing each palm in turn. "Ivy-mine."

coda

Five years later

Ivy TIED THE LAST OF THE RIBBONS around a
bunch of dried lavender and set a price tag sticker on
the bundle. She stretched, rolling her neck muscles,
and observed the winter display. The tourists would
love it. Jeb had told her this morning that his
woodshop in town was already seeing a huge rise in
visitors this season.

Every year, the land came back into itself, fresh,
green growth peeking out from the scars of old
magic. The forest folk had moved back into their
home, but Ivy and Archer had opted to stay in town
and help the people there come to a greater
understanding of the resource they'd very nearly lost.

Archer's forest tours had grown tremendously in
the last few years, taking townsfolk and tourists alike
into the forest for a display of magic and an education
on what the forest was, as well as what it wasn't…and

193

most of all, how to stay safe beneath the trees. More than ever, people wanted to visit this strange and infamous slice of land, and they needed a guide who knew its good side and its bad. In that, Archer was more of an expert than any ranger of the forest folk.

And with his base here in town, he provided a level of trustworthiness that other forest-folk guides, who didn't even have telephones, could not.

Over the door, a tiny golden bell rang as someone opened the door, a sweet, harmonious sound that never failed to make Ivy smile. There weren't a lot of the bells left these days. Tourists had bought up most of them, and scavengers claimed the rest, selling them far and wide as sleep aids and anti-depressants. She'd even seen a few hawked online as guaranteed ways to make your beloved stay with you forever.

That, of course, she couldn't argue with.

Even the wire that had once formed the bell lattice was worth money, and Sallie had made a fortune crafting healing jewelry from the metal that remained. Last summer, she'd moved someplace tropical. "I may be half-forest," she'd explained to Ivy, "but I think I need a change of scenery."

The quarry hadn't shut down, but for a while people feared it might, after Beemer's disappearance on the night the bells had begun to ring. Since no body was ever uncovered, and he'd never left a will, they placed the quarry in trust with the town until the mystery was solved. Deacon Ryder they'd found wandering the cliffs near the quarry a day later, babbling like a madman and embracing everyone he saw. Ivy heard somewhere that he'd set himself up in a city down south as a faith healer who cured through hugs.

At least he wasn't her problem anymore.

Many people did leave the town in those first few months, so afraid of the lies they'd been told about the forest. But more chose to stay, as if helping the forest folk that night had taught them more about humanity than three years of trying to define it ever could have.

Although the bells might have helped, too. Their sonorous chime rang through the town day and night for a week, drawing wonder and curiosity from all who heard the marvelous music. Then, at last, their song wound down, like an echo in a valley, and the bells went silent, hanging like ripe golden fruits from limb and pole.

Everyone had missed the sound. It wasn't long before people started claiming the bells for themselves, tiny pieces of peace and love to hold up against the darkness.

Ivy, it turned out, had her own.

Archer came into the kitchen, his arms full of evergreen boughs to decorate the mantel. He stomped the snow off his boots. "Counted twenty new trees this trip," he announced as he shrugged off his coat and grabbed the woven cuff of redbell from its hook near the door. "And I think someone made friends with every robin in the forest."

Behind him, a little wool hat bobbed just at the level of the countertops. "Hi, Mama!" the girl chirped, peeking up at her. Wild, red curls corkscrewed out from under her cap, but her eyes were pure black.

"Belle," Ivy warned. "What have you been up to?"

Archer dropped the boughs near the hearth and looked over. "Belle, my sweet. I told you to clean that up before we got home."

Belle hung her sweet head, playing idly with her necklace of braided redbell stalk. "Sorry, Papa. I love you." When she looked up again, her eyes were blue.

Ivy put her hands on her hips. "What were you showing her?"

Archer gave a guilty grin. "Levitation. How else was she going to talk to the robins up high?"

Ivy sighed. "She's going to scare off the tourists."

Belle laughed. "Just the scaredy cat ones."

River had assured Ivy that in time Belle would be able to cast a permanent glamor on her eyes, though Archer argued that she shouldn't have to. It was little more than a side-effect of the magic which still held her father in its grip on the night she was conceived. Belle's magic, Archer insisted, was nothing but light.

Ivy wondered if he'd still think that when Belle reached her teenaged, rebellious phase.

"Exactly." Archer slipped his arms around his wife's waist and kissed her. "And we don't want scaredy cats in our shop, do we?"

Ivy gave him a playful shove. "You're impossible."

"No," he corrected. "I'm magical. And so is Belle. And you're stuck with us."

"That's for sure."

Her own tiny Belle, ringing night and day as a constant reminder of the love she shared with Archer, the one that had brought him out of the darkness for good.

196

She bent down to address her daughter. "Want some cocoa?"

The girl grinned. "Yes, please!"

"Go wash your hands."

Belle scampered off to the bathroom and Archer leaned in again. "Don't I get any?"

"Only if you're good."

"Ivy-mine," he scoffed. "I'm always good. You know that."

This time when he kissed her, it was deep, and a rush of images flooded her mind, a heady mix of memories and promises of what they'd do later, after Belle was in bed and they had some time to themselves.

"*Always* good?" she asked, peppering kisses across his throat.

"All right," he admitted, and buried his face in her hair, breathing deep. "Mostly. But you love me, anyway."

Yes, Archer. Always.

~

"On, on they send, on without end,
Their joyful tone, to every home.
Ding, dong, ding, dong…"

author's note

This story was a long time in coming. Its earliest genesis was during a happy autumn night in a tropical hotel suite with dear writing friends Erica Ridley, Elissa Wilds, and C.L. Wilson, whose beautiful holiday anthology, *One Enchanted Season*, contains their inspiration from that evening.

I would also like to thank Justine Larbalestier, who first loved the idea from the other side of an ocean; Carrie Ryan, who discovered the right ending on a hike around a lake; and Holly Black, who saved the plot in the midst of a midnight blizzard.

For K.A. Linde, my beta reader extraordinaire, a crown of redbell for looking at a million covers and helping me find the perfect title, and for coining the phrase, "the reverse Angel" to describe Archer's plight. Gratitude to Heidi Joy Tretheway, Megan Erickson, Brenna Aubrey, and my other NAAU! friends for helping me with various aspects of production.

Thank you also to Lisa Christman, who stepped in at the last minute with a spectacular editing job. I'm so glad I got the chance to work with you.

And finally, thank you, reader. Stay warm. And be glad I didn't kill the dog.

http://vivdaniels.com